SANCTUARY

A MACY McVANNEL MYSTERY

REBECKA VIGUS

OPEN WINDOW

Livonia, Michigan

ALSO BY REBECKA VIGUS

Macy McVannel Novels
Rivers Edge
Crossing the Line

Other Novels
Out of the Flames
Secrets
Target of Vengeance

Non-Fiction
So You Think You Want to Be a Mommy?

Poetry
Only a Start and Beyond

Children's Books
Of Moonbeams and Fairies

Multi-Author Collections
In Creeps the Night

This book is dedicated to anyone who
has ever been verbally, emotionally, or physically abused.

CHAPTER ONE

Dani Montgomery always loved her grandparents' home with its nooks, crannies, and ghosts. When they died the house was left to her, and now she is making it her home.

She was twelve when she found the passage in the closet. She had not followed it far, but went in search of a flashlight to look later. When Dani finally went back she discovered a maze of hallways between the walls. She soon realized she could listen to conversations going on in different rooms. The day she discovered the chamber and old bathroom was the best.

The chamber contained old rickety beds. The mattresses had all but disintegrated, and the bathroom barely had plumbing. It had been a great hiding place for a young girl. She learned later the room had been used to hide slaves going north to Canada for freedom before and during the Civil War.

Dani knew the staff believed the house was haunted, but she knew different and was determined to put the old chamber to good use. The plan required the utmost in secrecy.

She returned to the main house after a trip into the old passage, to settle in permanently. A wall was being taken down between the den and the parlor which would now become her office. Heavy wooden doors would be added for privacy, but the parlor made a great reception area. She wanted to stay with the antique décor.

The kitchen had already been updated, along with the dining room. The size of the dining room had been so big Dani was able to cut it in half, separating it with French doors and creating a small living room. The staff had been against the changes at first; however most of them had watched her grow up and chose to let her have her way.

Ella, the housekeeper met her in the main hallway. "Miss Dani, where have you been? We were looking all over for you."

"I'm sorry, Ella, I was in the attic getting ready to root around and didn't hear you call," Dani replied.

"*That* building man said to call him when you were available," Ella said pouting.

"Just as soon as I find my phone," Dani said with a chuckle.

Ella walked away muttering, "The whole place is in an uproar and the child just laughs."

Dani smiled knowing Ella would complain even if she had been able to find Dani on the first try. It had been like that her entire life. Ella and Sam Miller lived in the gatehouse and worked at the main house. They had been here since before Dani was born. She loved them both and offered them the gatehouse for life.

She located her phone on the desk and punched the number for Brad Stevens' building company. Ella knew full well who Brad was, he and Dani had dated one summer when she was in high school, *a summer she hoped would never end.*

"Stevens' Construction Company, how may I direct your call?" asked a cheerful Maxie.

"Hey, Maxie, it's Dani. I understand Brad wants to talk to me."

"Sure, does. Hold on," she said.

"This is Brad," came a warm male voice after a few moments of waiting.

"Hi, Brad, it's Dani returning your call," she managed a calm reply even though she felt her heartbeat pick up.

"Dani, I have a couple things I need to go over with you. Will you be home later?" Brad asked.

"Sure why don't you come by for dinner?" she asked.

"Still serving at six?" he asked with a chuckle.

"Yes, but not black tie until Sunday," she laughed.

"I'll be there," he said and hung up the phone.

Dani had much to do before six. She headed to the kitchen to let Ella know there would be two for dinner.

SHOWERED AND DRESSED, Dani found herself nervous about meeting with Brad. Could she trust him enough with the rest of the renovations? She would wait to see what he wanted to talk about and make her decision then. She paced in the office waiting for him to arrive. She was so deep in thought; she jumped when the doorbell rang.

"I got it, Ella," she called walking to the door.

Ella appeared as Dani opened the door. Brad looked every bit as handsome as when they had been kids. He was holding a bouquet of yellow roses. Dani stepped aside so he could enter. Ella stepped forward saying, "I'll put those in water for you, Miss Dani." She took the flowers muttering as she walked away, "Opening the door like she is the help, harrumph."

Brad and Dani shared a chuckle before he said, "Some things never change. You look great, Dani."

"Thanks, you don't look too bad yourself. Join me in the office for a drink?" she asked leading the way.

Brad followed, taking in the changes she had been making. He liked what he saw. It also gave him time to get his own feelings under control.

"So, what'll you have?" she asked when they reached the bar area.

"Whatever you're having."

"Two seven-sevens, coming right up. Do you want to talk business now or after dinner?"

"How about after, I'd like to just enjoy the company for now," he answered with a wink.

"Okay, what shall we talk about?" Dani asked giving him a sly glance.

"You, your law practice, moving here, how you've been, just for starters," he said.

"Don't want much do you?" she asked smiling as she handed him his drink. "Let's see, me, I've not changed much, still looking to defend the underdog, my practice does well. Moving here is all I hoped for and more. I've been fine, thanks for asking. How'd I do?"

Brad looked at her but did not reply as he let her words sink in. Dani laughed and took a sip of her drink. "So now it's your turn."

"First, I didn't expect all the answers in one breath. Second, business is good. Third, I'm fine." Brad shifted his feet and stared into his glass before looking at her again. Finally, he asked, "Dani, why did we ever stop dating?"

She paused for a moment to take a sip of her drink wondering if he was serious. She glanced at him and answered quickly, "I think it had something to do with you graduating high school and going off to an apprenticeship with your uncle."

"I was an idiot," was his blunt statement. "How could I have just walked away from you?"

"I was two years younger and you were going to set the construction industry on its ear," she recalled. "Besides, I planned to be the next crusader to save the world and didn't have time for a man on a mission. I had my own dream to follow."

Brad laughed at her response. "That's one of the things I love about you. You can always put things in perspective. I've missed you, Dani."

"I've missed you too," she whispered.

Ella arrived to announce dinner was ready and wondered what she had interrupted. Dani took their empty glasses to the bar then they walked slowly to the dining room.

BRAD PULLED OUT a chair for Dani then took one across from her. As they ate their salads Brad said, "I like the changes. It makes the house modern yet, keeps the old family feel of the place."

"Good, because I have some more in mind," she said offhandedly hoping to gauge his reaction.

"I'm up for it. Just let me know what and when."

Ella brought out the main course, served them, set the bowl in the center of the table, and said, "Miss Dani, I put the dessert on the counter. If there's nothing else, I'll be going."

Dani smiled saying, "We have everything. You and Sam have a good evening."

She left muttering, "Fools don't even see what's right in front of them."

Brad and Dani stifled laughter until they heard the back door close. "Is she always muttering under her breath?" he asked.

"She has mumbled for as long as I can remember," Dani said. "It's what sets her apart from the new girl she's training. The girl has no personality and is afraid of her shadow."

"Is Ella retiring?" Brad inquired.

"Oh, heavens no, Ella will be carried out of here on her deathbed. It's just getting to be too much for her to do it alone anymore," Dani told him. "I'd love for her to retire and allow me to provide her with some help, but she'd never hear of it."

"Sam's still tending the grounds?"

"Of course, he too is training a couple of young guys," she said.

They finished the rest of dinner rehashing old memories and catching up on friends. When they finished eating, Dani took their plates to the kitchen and got dessert. "Do you want this here or in the office?" she asked coming through the door, holding a delicious blueberry crisp in one hand and a container of ice cream in the other.

"Here is fine. We don't need to upset Ella because we ate in your office," Brad said reaching for a plate. They ate their dessert laughing and talking between bites.

When they finished dessert, both took their plates and silverware to the kitchen. "I'm stuffed. Ella is still the best cook I know," Brad said.

"Yes, she is." Dani rinsed the dishes, set them in the dishwasher, and pushed the start button. She took down two coffee cups, put them with cream and sugar on a tray and then put the coffee pot on the tray.

"Let me carry the tray," Brad said taking the tray from her.

Dani let him and they went to her office. "What is so important?" she asked as she poured them each a cup of coffee.

"I wanted to be sure the job is what you wanted and you're happy with it," Brad whispered, he had taken a seat across from her desk.

"Why wouldn't I be? Things have been going very well," she told him trying to figure out what he was thinking and where it was leading.

"I haven't been on site as much as I'd hoped," he said while thinking *I've been avoiding you.*

"It looks like you gave specific enough instructions. I have no complaints," Dani assured him.

"I'm glad," Brad sounded relieved.

"Is there something I should know?" Dani asked still trying to find out what Brad was not saying.

"No, I just don't like to neglect my customers," Brad answered. "Tell me about the other renovations you mentioned."

Dani was surprised as she did not think he had been listening. "I told you I need some other renovations done, but they have to be done in secret," she started.

"What do you mean in secret?" he asked suddenly suspicious.

"I don't want anyone else to know. You'd have to do them yourself," she said.

"Is this illegal?" he asked.

"The renovations aren't. I wouldn't ask you to involve yourself if it were," she told him truthfully.

"Okay, I'm in. What do you need done?"

"I'm going to show you where the ghosts live. Did you bring your sense of adventure with you?" She smiled as she rose.

"Dani, you're always an adventure," he told her rising to join her.

If he was surprised when she handed him a flashlight, his face didn't show it. Dani led the way upstairs to a closet in the hallway. She opened the door and walked in, Brad following her. She tapped on the back wall about midway up and the wall slid open. Brad said nothing but turned on his flashlight and followed her.

Dani led the way until they reached the chamber. They had been up and down stairs, followed twists and turns until Brad knew he was lost. "This is it," she said.

"What is this place?" he asked looking around.

"This is where the escaped slaves were kept until they could be moved to the next stop on their way north. I used it to hide in when I was a kid," she answered.

"What do you want me to do with it?" Brad asked surveying the remnants of the room and wondering why Dani didn't just close it off.

"For one thing I need lighting throughout the tunnel. The bathroom is in serious need of updating, I'd like to paint this room, put in bunk beds, a small refrigerator, and maybe even a cook top," she told him.

"What are you planning to do down here?" he asked.

"I can't tell you, Brad. I just need to know if you can do this for me?" she asked.

"I can but I'm not sure I like it. Where does that go?" he asked indicating a tunnel off to the right.

"Follow me if you dare," she said leading the way. Brad pointed his flashlight after Dani's retreating shape even as the hairs on his neck stood on end. If she was running true to form, Dani had a scheme of some kind and he was going to get sucked into it.

They emerged from the cave not more than twenty yards from the river they swam in as children. The dock was in need of repair, but the big oak still stood sentry over their favorite picnic spot. Brush had grown up making the entrance to the cave more secluded.

"Wow, how long have you known about this?" Brad asked.

"Since before I met you," she answered. "I've never told anyone."

"I bet it was a great hiding place for a kid."

"It was," she answered. "Now I'm going to put it to a better use."

"Promise me you won't be doing anything illegal," Brad said with a worried look on his face.

"I'm an officer of the law for goodness sake," she said frustrated. "I'm not likely to be smuggling or anything along those lines."

Brad sighed. Knowing Dani and her penchant for trouble, he just knew this would not be good. At least by doing the work, he could keep tabs on her for a while. Whatever she had in mind, he would do anything to protect her from harm.

"Sure I can do it, but it will have to be after hours, when I get off work," he told her. "I might be able to bring stuff up the river and unload here."

"The first thing you'll need to do is fix the old dock," she said. She had been sure he would take the job and smiled at how easy he had been to convince. Brad looked at the dock while assessing the materials he would need. He also wanted to frame a door inside the cave. It wouldn't do for neighborhood kids to stumble into whatever Dani planned.

"I can have the guys fix the dock up tomorrow morning. It'll be ready for me by evening," Brad told her.

CHAPTER TWO

Brad was not surprised to see Dani waiting on the river bank for him the next night at dusk. He had loaded a small motorboat with electrical wire, plumbing supplies and as much wood as he could safely haul. She came out onto the dock to help him secure the boat.

"Dinner is ready and we can eat as soon as we unload," she said smiling.

Brad watched her as she lifted things onto a wagon she brought to help with hauling. He quickly lifted the things she could not, the wagon was loaded and pulled into the cave in no time. They slipped into the house through the closet with Dani giggling as they made their way to the kitchen.

Ella looked at them with disapproval but set their dinner on the table and left the room. "Some folks don't know how to behave," she muttered as she left.

Her comment sent Dani into peals of laughter. Brad loved her laugh. He loved everything about the saucy lawyer, including her bubbly personality, blue eyes that looked like bottomless pools, and her unruly blonde curls. When he realized he was staring at her, he focused on his food.

After dinner Dani drove Brad to town and dropped him off at his office. "I'll have coffee when you get there in the morning."

Brad smiled, "Thanks see you then."

AS PROMISED, DANI was waiting with coffee when he arrived before the sun. He took a cup from her and headed toward the closet. He had been thinking about how to wire the tunnels.

"We need to tap into this light switch and put one higher up that will always be on. Then the lights can be controlled," Brad told her.

"Whatever you need to do," Dani replied. "Should I have this closet emptied?"

"No, I don't want anyone wondering why we need to work in here." Brad was quick to answer.

"Makes sense I just thought it might be easier to work if it was empty," Dani quipped.

Brad took out his flashlight letting it play over the walls of the tunnel. "I should be able to get up to the ceiling from here. Give me two hours and come find me. I want to be gone before everyone gets here."

"Sure thing," Dani smiled and left him to work.

BRAD WAS COMING out of the closet when Dani arrived. "Great timing," she said.

He handed her his keys. "Take my truck into town. I'll take the boat back. Meet me at my office and I'll bring you home."

She took his keys, watching as he headed back down the tunnel to the boat then headed for the truck. She missed spending time with Brad. The feelings she had for him were still there.

They met at his office and she returned his keys. They rode in silence back to Dani's. Brad wondered if she had any idea the effect she had on him. He missed her spontaneity. *To be honest, he missed everything about her, her laughter, the way it felt right holding her, and her propensity for finding trouble in things which for anyone else would be simple.* Brad found himself smiling.

Getting out of the truck Brad gently took Dani's arm turning her to face him, "Promise me you will be careful."

"I will," she replied reaching up to brush a stray lock of hair from his forehead. Turning she reminded him, "Dinner is at six."

CHAPTER THREE

T he next morning Dani went to town to check out all the new renovations Brad had made to the downtown area. She looked and felt like a tourist, because so much had changed. Dani admired the improvements Brad had made. As she made her way to the city offices, she found herself in awe of how different things looked. There were white pillars and gingerbread trim on the buildings and the central courtyard had been transformed to look like a park from an 1800's painting. The quaint Victorian feeling the town was known for still remained. She thought *Brad has done well for himself,* as she drove back home daydreaming about him.

Thinking of Brad made Dani smile. *She remembered how devastated she had been when he went off to work and never contacted her again. His dark curly hair with the lock that kept falling over his brow and general good looks had captivated her. His dark brown eyes seemed to look into her soul. He had always been a gentleman, and followed her unquestioningly on her many escapades the summer they spent together. She shook herself from her reverie.*

BRAD ARRIVED PROMPTLY at six for dinner carrying a duffle bag. Ella eyed it suspiciously as she told him, "Miss Dani is in the den."

"Thank you, Ella," he said as he headed in toward Dani's office.

Dani was just finishing a brief and sending it to her printer as Brad walked in. He loved watching her work. She had a pencil shoved behind her ear and was concentrating on the materials coming off her printer. She had not yet noticed him and when she did, she jumped.

"I didn't hear you come in," she said catching her breath.

"No problem, I was enjoying the view," he answered smiling. "What are you working on?"

"A brief for one of my cases," she replied. "I was downtown today. You did a wonderful job with the renovations there."

I'm glad you like them," he said with pride. "I spent enough hours with the City Council going over what they wanted and keeping them from constant changes." He shook his head at the memory.

"Let's have dinner I'm starved," Dani said quickly changing the subject.

Dinner was less formal than the first night had been. Dani had requested a light fare and no dessert. She knew Brad would want to get to work so he could get home. She really had him pushing his limits on this project.

They talked about old times and old friends then Brad made his way to the closet. "Sure you don't need some help?" Dani offered.

"Not until I get the wiring done," Brad replied. "Should be done to the chamber tonight," he added as he made his way into the tunnel.

Left on her own, Dani went back to her office to reread the brief she had written.

Brad was a dusty mess two hours later when he appeared in her doorway.

"Want a shower before you hit the road?" she asked looking him up and down.

"Would be nice, if it's not too much trouble," he replied.

"Follow me."

Anywhere, Brad thought to himself as he followed Dani back up the stairs. She found him some towels and left him to shower and clean up.

Ten minutes later he was back in her office. "This is much better, don't you think?" he asked.

She walked to where he was standing taking in the fresh scrubbed scent of him. "Oh, yes," she sighed.

"Wiring to the chamber room is complete. We should think about putting up some insulation before we drywall to help muffle any sounds you might make while down there," he suggested.

Dani nodded. "Whatever you think is best," she said distractedly.

"Are you ever going to tell me what you plan to do there?"

Looking at him, Dani knew she would have to tell him sooner or later. Later she decided. "Not yet."

"I guess I'll have to live with it," Brad said with resignation. Dani had her own way of doing things. "Then I'm off. I'll be back tomorrow for dinner." He smiled at her as he walked to the door and let himself out.

DANI FOUND HERSELF daydreaming about the summer she and Brad had spent together. *They started dating when he asked her to prom. She had been thrilled. She had watched him off and on for most of her sophomore year of high school, trying to figure out how to get his attention without being forward as her mother called it. He was captain of the football and baseball teams and she was surprised he did not play basketball, even though he attended the games. Then there he was one day after school standing at her locker. She smiled up at him and said,*

"Excuse me." He had moved so she could get into the locker but she was very aware of his presence.

"Can I walk you to your bus?" he asked shyly.

She remembered replying; "Sure," as if it were something he did daily. Her heart was fluttering so loudly she was sure everyone could hear it.

On the way out to the bus Brad took her hand and pulled her to face him, "Dani, I've been working up the courage to do this for a week, so please don't interrupt." She just nodded and he went on, "I'd like you to be my date for prom."

Dani knew her heart had stopped beating. He had to work up courage to ask her to prom? Wow was all she could think. She smiled at him and said, "I'd be happy to be your date."

He picked her up and twirled her around before setting her on the ground, and then he took her hand and walked her to the bus.

It had been the beginning. Brad had spent every moment he could with Dani. Most of the time was spent here at her grandparents. When her parents had died in a car accident right after school got out, Dani had moved in with her grandparents. Brad had stayed in the guest room to be there when Dani needed him. They had talked for hours, swam in the river, run through the woods and fields. He was her knight in shining armor. Just as suddenly as he came into her life he was gone. He had told her the week before school started he was going to his uncle's to become an apprentice in his carpentry shop. Dani had been devastated but she said nothing, just asked him to write and stop in when he was home. He agreed, but he never had.

Dani did not think she would ever get over him. She had dug into her studies and graduated in the top five in her class. Then she had been accepted to college and had taken advance placement tests for several of her classes. Her major was undetermined when she went off to college. She just knew she wanted to help people. Now here he was back in her life again.

The time had come to tell him what her plans were for the tunnel and chamber rooms. She hoped he would support her.

CHAPTER FOUR

The next night found Brad back at Dani's. He finished the wiring, framed, and hung the door at the mouth of the cave. He made a dimmer switch for the hallway in from the cave opening. When he finished he showered then went in search of Dani.

Brad found Dani in her office with two seven-sevens already made. She handed him one and took a seat behind her desk. He sat in front of it wondering if she was finally going to tell him what she planned for the secret room. He did not have long to wait.

Dani took a drink and looked at Brad. Finally she said, "I'm going to tell you a story. It has a lot to do with who I am today and why we are working so hard on the hidden room."

Brad eased back in his chair, nodded, and took a sip of his drink. He was going to give her all the time she needed.

She handed him a photo. In it were three young women, all beautiful. Dani was in the center.

"Those were my roommates in college," she started. "The one on my left is Macy McVannel; she's a police detective in Rivers Edge. The other is Michelle Avery. She was vibrant, talented, and I expected her to be the most successful of the three of us."

"You said was," Brad started. Dani held up a finger and he stopped.

"We did everything together until Michelle met Adam Savoy," the venom in her voice startled Brad. "He took over her life, cutting her off from everyone; Macy, me, her family, and anyone who tried to talk to her. She moved in with him before Thanksgiving our sophomore year. Macy and I did everything we could to talk her out of it."

Dani sighed remembering. "About two weeks later she joined us for lunch. Even the make-up could not hide the bruises. Adam was beating her. Macy and I convinced her to move back with us. We were relieved when she agreed. Things got worse from there. He stalked her, tried grabbing her off the street, and called all the time. Finally we convinced her to get a PPO-personal protection order-he blew when he was served. We had already changed the phone number, so he couldn't call."

Taking a big drink Dani gathered her thoughts before saying anymore. Brad could see she was fighting tears, but he said nothing. Then she began again, "One night just before exams, Macy and I were studying in the library, Michelle had to work and was going to join us when she got out. We got worried when she didn't show up and we couldn't reach her at home or work. Macy decided we needed to go check on her. She said something about having a bad feeling. So, we packed up and walked to our apartment. The police and an ambulance were outside when we arrived. We were just in time to see a person brought out on a stretcher, but with the people around we could not see who. An officer stopped us as we tried to get closer. When we told him we lived there and were worried about our roommate, he told us to wait. He returned with a detective. It was Michelle on the stretcher. She'd been beaten. The nice detective drove us to the hospital, where they had taken Michelle right into surgery. We gave him the number so he could call her parents. We also told him everything about Michelle's relationship with Adam

Savoy. Left in the waiting room, Macy and I cried as we waited to hear about Michelle." Tears began streaming down her face.

Brad set his drink on her desk and walked around it to take her in his arms. He held her while she cried. "I get the idea, Dani, you don't need to tell me anymore," he whispered.

She struggled to pull herself together, "Yes, I do. You need to know it all so you will understand what I want to do." She stepped out of Brad's arms giving herself some distance. Looking at him she continued, "Michelle died on the operating table before her parents could arrive. Adam Savoy was picked up as he arrived at home with her blood all over him. He beat her to death." She gulped for air as she said the last, as her own tears subsided she continued, "It's why I became an attorney. I am going to use the chamber and the tunnel to help battered women escape from their tormentors. I will allow them to bring their children. It's going to become a modern day Underground Railroad." She stopped then, looking at Brad for reaction.

"Is it legal?" he asked.

"I don't know. I just know there are some women who have no means of escape and the courts cannot always protect them. There is a group who does this kind of thing, but they are secretive about it. I've been in contact with them," she said, her blue eyes pleading with him to understand.

"I will do whatever I can to help," he told her moving once again to take her in his arms. He held her feeling her relax and her breathing return to normal.

She whispered, "Thank you."

"Come on," he said, "Walk me to the door."

Arm-in-arm they walked to Dani's front door. He turned to say good-night and pulled her gently into his arms kissing her with all the passion he could. He left her saying, "Sleep well, Sprite."

Dani closed the door and watched from the window as Brad walked to his truck. *Sprite, he called me Sprite.* She smiled wondering if he remembered the long ago nickname or if it was just something to say.

ALL THE WAY home Brad wondered if he had messed up again, *Sprite, the nickname he had given her all those years ago. Would she remember? Would she even care? Part of him wanted to turn the truck around and go back to her.* He would not give in. This was too important for both of them.

DANI FLOATED UP the stairs to her room. *Sprite, he remembered. She had longed to hear him call her by the pet name he had given her so long ago.* Finding her nightgown Dani put it on, crawled beneath the covers, and fell into a dreamless sleep.

Sunlight was flooding through the window when she awoke the next morning. The tantalizing scents from the kitchen had drifted all the way to Dani's room. She was up, showered, dressed, and on her way down the stairs quickly.

Ella looked up from some dough she was kneading as Dani entered. "I have some quiche and tarts warming for you," she said as Dani took down a cup and poured some coffee.

"You are the best, Ella," Dani said as she kissed the woman's cheek on her way to the oven to retrieve her breakfast.

"Sleeping late is not like you," Ella commented continuing to knead.

"I had to do some late work," Dani answered as she sat at the table and began to eat. "I'll be interviewing two women today for the office position."

Ella slammed the dough onto the cupboard. "Home is a home, not a place of work," she muttered.

Dani chuckled between bites, "Ella, I can do both here and save money on office rent in town."

"Saving money and bringing in riff-raff," was her muttered response.

Smiling Dani finished her breakfast and took a second cup of coffee to the office with her. She had settled at her desk, when Chloe, the new girl knocked.

Looking up, Dani smiled, "Yes, Chloe?"

"There is a young woman," Chloe started as a young woman pushed her way into Dani's office.

"It's fine, Chloe," Dani told her. The girl backed out and closed the door.

"I'm Dani Montgomery," she said reaching out her hand.

"Yeah, I'm Gail Snell," was the reply. Gail took a seat and continued, "I'm here for the job."

Dani sat looking the girl up and down. Her hair was brown; at least Dani thought it was. The blue, red, and green stripes made it hard to tell. The neon green tank top and blue jeans were not impressive. Dani reached for the file on her desk. "What made you apply for this position?"

Snapping her gum Gail answered, "I thought someday I might like to be a lawyer and this would help me decide."

"What types of positions have you had in the past?"

"I've done baby-sitting and took some classes in cosmetology," she answered.

"Do you have any kind of office training?"

"Why would I need to? Isn't this an on the job training situation?" Gail asked.

Dani answered, "I am looking for someone who has office skills. I need someone who is capable of setting up an office and keeping it running."

"Shoot, I thought running the office was your job," Gail said looking appalled. "I just wanted to answer the phones and get the gossip on folks."

"I'm sorry I wasted your time," Dani replied. "I don't think this is the position for you."

"If you're going to be snotty about it, I don't think so either," Gail stood and left the room, leaving the door open.

Dani heard the front door slam as the girl left. *What a twit. She really thought she could snoop through my cases?* Dani just shook her head.

Fifteen minutes later Chloe arrived at the door with another woman for Dani to interview. "Miss Dani, another woman for you."

"Thank you, Chloe, that will be all," Dani said as she stood to greet the newcomer. "Mrs. Maureen Beckett?" She again held her hand out in greeting.

Mrs. Beckett took her hand and shook it warmly, "Thank you for considering me, Miss Montgomery." She was mid-fifties dressed in a dove grey suit with a pale green blouse. Her greying hair was pulled away from her face.

"Please, have a seat and call me Dani." Both women sat. "Tell me something about your experience," Dani prompted.

"I have worked for Able Maynard for the past fifteen years," Maureen told her. "If he hadn't had a stroke I'd probably still be there."

"You are not afraid of setting up a new office?"

"Heavens, no," Maureen answered. "I'd be delighted to help you set-up. This is a beautiful location."

"Thank you, Mrs. Beckett. I wanted it to reflect the home I grew up in, while using it as my office."

"If we are going to work together, you need to call me, Maureen."
"Agreed if you will call me, Dani."

"I'm not sure I could, but maybe Miss Dani?" Maureen questioned.

Dani laughed, "You will work out famously. My housekeeper has called me, Miss Dani, all my life. Let's look at your office."

Together they walked into the parlor area. "I love the décor here," Maureen commented. "This will be a delightful place to work."

"When you come in Monday morning, please go through the supplies I have and let me know what you still need," Dani told her.

"I will be here early Monday, so we can open for business exactly at nine," Maureen assured her.

"We will do just fine together," Dani told her. "I look forward to seeing you on Monday." She walked Maureen to the door and out onto the porch.

"Where would you like me to park?" Maureen asked as they walked down the steps.

Dani paused looking out over the lawn, she had not considered parking. "Why don't you pull on the parking pad," she said indicating the paved pad at the side of the house.

"Perfect, I'll see you on Monday." Maureen walked to her car and drove away.

Dani looked around the yard wondering if she should put in some kind of parking lot and how it could be done without destroying the beauty surrounding her home.

CHAPTER FIVE

Dani was waiting on the porch when Brad drove in. He found himself smiling when he caught sight of her. She bounded off the porch toward his truck.

"I'm going to like being greeted this way," he told her as he scooped her into his arms.

She laughed and kissed his nose. "I need your advice."

"Hmmm, sounds ominous," he chuckled putting her down.

"Look around here, how am I going to put in a parking lot and not destroy the beauty of the yard?" she moaned.

Brad glanced around the yard then back at Dani, "I think I can find a way to take care of it," he assured her.

"I knew you'd have an answer," she smiled up at him. She grabbed his hand and started toward the house, "Let's get food, I've been worried about this all day and I'm starved."

Brad laughed as he followed her into the house. They ate and talked. When they were done both of them headed to the hidden chamber.

"Dani," Brad began, "I need to know if you are planning to have people in this area."

She looked at him and took a deep breath, "I am. I know first-hand the justice system cannot always protect those it needs to. I am going to offer this as a stopping point to freedom for abused women and their children."

There was silence for a moment then Brad spoke, "I need to put some insulation in before we can drywall. I think tonight I will see what needs to be done for plumbing, figure out how much insulation I need and measure for bathroom needs."

Dani was still not sure if he approved or not, but she walked to him and gave him a big hug. "I won't get in your way and distract you." Then she turned and left through the tunnel to the closet.

Not distract me? She must be nuts to think she doesn't distract me, Brad thought. He remembered the summer they had spent together. Dani had agreed to be his date to prom. He knew he was the luckiest guy in the world. After the prom, they had started dating regularly. They came out here because Dani's parents were on a trip and she was staying with her grandparents.

They swam in the river, hiked in the woods, climbed trees, and maybe he even slayed a dragon or two. It was idyllic. He fell in love with the girl he nicknamed, Sprite. Her blonde hair in a ponytail, wet from swimming, or down and curled when they were going somewhere. In all her different moods, he had fallen hard.

Then came the news her parents had died. Dani was devastated. He had refused to leave her side. Her grandparents had put him in the guest room and he had stayed with her until she fell asleep then walked down the hall to find rest for himself. His heart broke for her.

At the end of the summer his uncle offered him an apprenticeship in construction. Brad leaped at the chance. He would be able to take classes at the community college near his uncle in drafting. Telling Dani was the hardest thing he ever did. He wanted her to be free to date. In his heart, he did not want her dating anyone; he wanted her waiting for him. He had cut all ties with her and pursued a career.

He had kept track of her and knew she was Valedictorian of her class. He had been there at her graduation even if she did not know. He knew which college she had attended. He even knew when she passed her bar exam to become a lawyer. What he did not know is if she had found someone new to love. He was afraid to find out.

Now here he was remodeling a secret passage in the old house because she had some new scheme to get him involved in. Yes, Dani was still a distraction and he still loved her beyond reason.

Shaking himself out of his reverie, Brad set to work measuring for the insulation he would need and the sound proofing he would put in before the drywall. When he finished he walked to the end of the tunnel to check on the door he had already installed. It was sound. He did not want kids to wander in and find the chamber.

A couple of hours later, Brad found himself watching Dani as she read through a book looking for something. He waited until she noticed he was there.

"Have you been waiting long?" she asked looking up.

"Just a few minutes," he answered smiling, "I have all the measurements I need and all the electrical wiring done."

She came from behind her desk to hug him. "Thank you, I know this has been a lot to ask of you."

"Think nothing of it," Brad replied hugging her back.

They walked to the door and he kissed her before heading home.

CHAPTER SIX

After weeks of looking through law books, Dani still could not find where this project was illegal. Nor could she find where it was legal. She knew she was going to be treading a fine line. She wondered if she could pull it off. It was Friday, Brad had told her to get dressed up he was taking her out for dinner to a fancy restaurant between here and Rivers Edge. Some place called the Log Cabin Inn. *It didn't sound fancy to her.*

Dani showered and curled her hair. Then she chose a light blue dress she knew would bring out her eyes. She put on a sapphire necklace and grabbed a white shawl. *This will have to do,* she thought as she started down the stairs. She heard the doorbell ring and knew Brad had arrived.

Ella let Brad in and he looked up the staircase as Dani made her way down. The woman was a vision in blue. She was even more beautiful than she had been the night of prom.

"You look gorgeous," he said simply.

Dani smiled and responded, "You don't look half bad yourself." All the while she noticed his navy suit and light blue shirt. Ironic it almost matched her dress as if it had been planned. She pirouetted to give him the full effect.

"Come on let's get out of here," Brad said. As she drew closer he whispered, "Or I might get us both in trouble."

Laughter bubbled from Dani as they walked to his car. She was impressed with his jet black sports car.

They drove to the restaurant and as they were waiting for valet parking, Dani squealed, "I'll be right back, and leaped from the car."

Stunned, Brad followed her with his eyes as she approached a beautiful brunette on the arm of a gentleman. The brunette broke from her date to embrace Dani. Brad thought the woman looked familiar, but could not place her. When his car was taken by the valet, he joined the trio on the sidewalk.

Dani turned to him saying, "Brad, this is my college roommate, Macy McVannel and her date, Eli Patterson. Macy, Eli, this is Brad Stevens."

They all shook hands and Eli said, "Why don't you join Macy and I tonight?"

"We wouldn't want to impose," was Brad's polite reply.

"No imposition at all and it will be nice for the ladies," Eli prompted.

Dani looked at him with those big blue eyes and he knew he would give in. "Sure, why not?"

The smile Dani rewarded him with was enough to take his breath away. He had wanted a quiet romantic evening, but if this is what it turned out to be, he could live with it.

The four walked in together, Eli said to the maître d, "Mr. Stevens and Ms. Montgomery will be joining us tonight."

"As you wish, Mr. Patterson, right this way." The maître d led them to a private dining room and uncorked the champagne already on ice. He poured them each a glass and retired from the room.

"I hope you don't mind, but we ordered ahead," Eli told them.

"No, problem," Brad replied.

Macy took Dani by the hand and the two headed out to the private garden. Leaving the men to entertain each other.

"So, have you known Dani a long time?" Eli asked.

"A life time," Brad responded, "and I was stupid enough to let her go once. I won't make the mistake again." His gaze wandered to the two women in the garden.

"I understand," Eli replied. "I will wait a lifetime for Macy to come to my way of thinking."

"So, what do you do?" Brad asked.

"I'm a captain in the state police. I run the missing child division. And you?

"I own Stevens Construction in Willow Bend."

The women returned and the men seated them as salad was served. Conversation continued as Macy and Dani caught up with each other. Eli and Brad just smiled. Dinner came and went and Eli suggested dancing in the garden. The foursome made their way to the patio and as if on cue the violins began a waltz. The two couples glided through the dance and a couple more as if in a world of their own.

It was Macy who said, "I need a break and I know dessert will be waiting."

Dani laughed and followed her inside. Sure enough dessert was there waiting. As the couples ate and talked, the evening wound down. They were getting ready to leave when Brad said to Eli, "How much do I owe you for this?"

Chuckling Eli replied, "It's on the house."

"No, really," Brad insisted, "you weren't expecting Dani and I, so part of the bill is mine."

Eli said, "I own the restaurant, it really is on the house."

"Wow, thanks," Brad said and put out a hand to shake Eli's.

The women had drifted to the patio to say their good-byes. Brad looked at Eli and said, "I hope we will see each other again."

"If those two have their way, and they will, I'm sure we will be seeing a lot of each other."

Sharing a laugh the men went to fetch their ladies and head for home.

DANI LEANED BACK into the seat and looked at Brad, "Thank you for letting us join them. I know it's not what you had planned."

"It was a great evening. I like both Eli and Macy," he assured her.

"I so hope this works out for her," Dani said. "She doesn't have much luck where men are concerned. Her last fiancé died in the line of duty."

"Wow, and she is involved with another officer. Tell me did Macy go into law enforcement after Michelle?" Brad asked.

"Yes, we were both determined to make the justice system work," she answered.

"I'm proud of what you do, Dani," he told her.

She smiled and said, "Thank you."

They were silent for the rest of the ride both lost in their own thoughts. When they pulled into Dani's Brad walked her to the door. She looked out on the land now hers and said, "I never thought I'd want to come back here."

Brad hugged her from behind and replied, "I'm glad you did."

She leaned into him because it felt right. They stood there several minutes. Then Dani asked, "Do you want to come in?"

"I can't, Dani, it would only lead to trouble," he answered turning her to face him. "I want you. I need you. I love you, but I want to do it right this time." He took her in his arms kissing her with a passion she did not know existed, then he put her down and said, "Sleep well, Sprite, I'll see you tomorrow for breakfast. Have the coffee ready."

Dani stood on the porch and watched him drive away. *He told me he loves me and wants me, what on earth did I do wrong?*

As he drove away Brad cursed himself for being an idiot. *Dani all but invited him to stay and he turned her down. He wanted her to know he was for real. He was not walking out like he did all those years ago. But the hurt on her face, broke his heart. It had been a big step for her to ask him to stay, he knew. Breakfast couldn't come soon enough.*

As his tail lights disappeared, Dani let herself into the house and made her way to her bedroom. She stripped off her clothes, put on a nightgown, and crawled into bed. There she thought about Macy and Eli and how happy they seemed. She wondered if she would ever have a similar feeling. She loved Brad; she had for as long as she could remember. Part of the reason she had moved back was in hopes of seeing him again. Well, she was seeing him, but she sure did not feel like things were going as she planned. Somewhere while pondering all of this, she fell into a deep and dreamless sleep.

CHAPTER SEVEN

Dani dragged herself out of bed and into blue jeans and a t-shirt. She pulled her hair back in a ponytail, then made her way to the kitchen. She found the coffee pot already on and a note on the cupboard.

Miss Dani,

I knew you would be out late last night. Preheat the oven to 350 and in the refrigerator you will find a quiche ready to go in. Cook it for about 35 minutes.

Ella

Smiling, she did as the note instructed. Wondering as she did so, if Ella had expected Brad to be here in the morning, too. Well, he would be here soon enough. Dani busied herself setting the table and getting ready for breakfast when she heard the doorbell ring. She had expected to see Brad, but was greeted by a huge bouquet of flowers. Laughing she took them from him and together they headed for the kitchen. Dani put the flowers in water and then served breakfast.

As Dani did the dishes, Brad headed to the hidden chamber. He spent the next two hours doing rough plumbing so he could put in a sink, toilet, and shower. Then he went to work on the insulation. He had decided to insulate all the way to the outside door.

Dani showed up at lunch with a picnic basket. "Let's go sit by the river," she suggested.

Brad was ready for a break and agreed. They walked through the tunnel to the river bank. There Brad washed up in the river. They spread out a blanket under a shade tree and ate lunch. It was a lighthearted affair. Dani took out the lunch she packed. They talked about dinner the night before, the weather, before Dani pondered aloud, "I wonder if anyone will ever build across the river?"

"Would you like someone to build there?" Brad asked.

"I don't think so," she answered. "For one thing they'd probably be nosy and want to know about my river activity. Something which could potentially put those I'm trying to save in jeopardy."

Brad smiled, "I guess you don't have to worry then."

Looking at him sideways, she asked, "What do you mean?"

"I own the property across the river," he replied.

"When did you buy it?"

"A long time ago," he answered. "I hoped I'd be able to build and get a glimpse of you here now and then."

"Why? You didn't have to buy the land to see me," she told him.

"I was afraid you'd find someone who would know how to love you better than I did and marry him," he answered honestly. "I at least wanted a chance to see you even if it was from a distance."

Dani looked at him as if he had grown horns. "There has never been anyone else in my life. Yes, I have dated once in a while, but they never measured up to you."

"Seriously, Dani?" he asked. "I need to know because I've been waiting a long time for you to come home so I could make up all my past mistakes and we could start again."

Dani lunged at him toppling him onto the blanket. "I've never been more serious in my life." She kissed him then. Laughing when she finally let him come up for air. "I have a confession," she told him. "I came home hoping you were still single and maybe we could start out fresh."

"You did?"

"How do you think you got the remodeling job?" she asked with a twinkle in her eye.

"I thought maybe my reputation as a decent, honest builder had something to do with it," he admitted.

"Ha, no conceit there," she countered laughing.

"Dani, why didn't you just tell me?" Brad asked.

"I was afraid you'd be married with children and I didn't want to get in your way," she whispered.

"I've spent days avoiding you and nights dreaming about you," Brad told her. "I wanted to do everything right this time."

"You have done everything right," she told him.

"From now on no games," Brad stated. "We are up front in our relationship and let it run where it will."

"Agreed," she said with a smile and started gathering up their lunch. Brad leaned in to help and kissed her cheek.

"In case you haven't gotten my message, I love you," he whispered and helped her up.

"Loud and clear," she replied. "I love you, too."

Together they entered the tunnel. Brad to do some more work and Dani to take care of lunch remnants and busy herself.

DANI HUMMED TO herself as she took care of their lunch all the while thinking *It could work. Brad and I could have a future here at the Willows. I only hope he means what he says.* The niggling hurt from long ago crept in to try and steal her happiness. She finished in the kitchen and headed for her office. She had work to do, if she was going to be successful on her newest mission.

In the hidden chamber, Brad whistled while he worked. *Dani still loves me. There is a chance I can make up for being an idiot. I want her to be my wife and spend my life loving her.* The thought made him happy and he put all his energy into finishing her secret project.

He wandered upstairs, took a shower and went to look for Dani. He had promised her a cook out at his home. It was going on five and he still had to get the grill going. He found her in her office pouring over law books again. It took his breath away to see the intensity in her face. He wondered what it would be like to see her in a court room in action.

Sensing Brad in the room, Dani looked up and smiled. "Done for the day?"

"Yep, I came to collect you for dinner."

"What time is it?" she asked.

"About five, are you ready to go?"

"I sure am," she said closing the book and getting up. He waited as she came to him then took her hand and they walked to his truck.

On the way to Brad's she asked, "So, what did you think of Eli Patterson?"

"I like him. Did you know he's not only a police officer, but he owns the restaurant?"

"Macy didn't mention he owned the restaurant," Dani admitted. "She is concerned he will be hurt or killed in the line of duty." She turned to look at Brad asking, "Did he tell you how they met?"

"Nope, just told me what he did. He's captain of the missing children division of the state police," Brad's voice held admiration. "I don't think I'd want to deal with kids missing and distraught parents."

"Wow, Macy didn't tell me," she answered in awe. "She told me he was assigned to protection duty for Macy and a couple she had been protecting. They spent late nights talking and getting to know one another before he got shot helping one of the people they were protecting."

"What an amazing story," he said. "It will be something to tell their grandchildren."

"Whoa, slow down," Dani told him. "Macy tends to overthink things. Don't marry her off just yet. I get the feeling she cares deeply for him, but is gun shy from losing Craig in the line of duty."

Brad countered with, "Maybe Eli will give up police work and just keep the restaurant."

"It's a thought," she agreed. "We'll have to see how it plays out."

They arrived at Brad's, ending any further discussion. He had a small bungalow at the end of a long winding driveway.

"This is close to heaven," Dani said admiringly.

"Thanks, I think of it as my retreat," he told her.

"How many acres do you have here?" she asked.

"Only five," he answered. "With this and the river front property I have my hands full."

"It's one way to keep you out of trouble," she laughed.

They went inside where the floor plan was open and the rooms were light and airy. Dani admired the natural woodworking he had done. As Brad busied himself getting the grill going, Dani wandered through the house. It had a strong masculine feeling but was not overwhelmingly rustic. She made her way to the deck where Brad had steaks on the grill. He poured her an iced tea and she sat at the table looking over the backyard. It was peaceful here. She understood why Brad liked it, so did she. It was not the old house she now called home, but it had a charm of its own.

Dinner was a quiet affair. As they were finishing up Brad said, "Turn slowly and look over your right shoulder." Following his directions she did and discovered a doe and fawn feeding at the tree line. She smiled watching them. As they faded into the woods, Brad and Dani cleaned up. Dani washed the dishes and Brad dried.

Coming up behind her after putting the last of the dishes away, he wrapped his arms around her and asked, "Do you want to stay tonight or do you want me to take you home?"

"Would you be terribly disappointed if I told you, I think I want to go home?"

"Not at all," he assured her kissing the top of her head.

Dani wiggled in his arms until she was facing him. "Soon," she told him as she leaned in to kiss him.

On the ride back to her house, Dani sat in the middle of the truck and leaned against Brad's shoulder. Feeling content for the first time in years, she savored the moment.

Brad put his arm around her shoulders and pulled her close to him. It felt right to just be holding her. The ride back was too short for his liking. He walked Dani to the front door. Before she could open it he pulled her to him for a soul shattering kiss. Then he left her standing on the porch and headed to his truck and home.

Dani let herself in and made her way up the stairs to her bed.

CHAPTER EIGHT

Up early, showered, making a quick breakfast, dressed in her pajamas and robe, so she could get ready for church, Dani heard a car pull into the drive. Puzzled she carried her coffee with her as she made her way to the front door. Brad was getting out of his car wearing dress pants and carrying a sport coat. He smiled when he saw her. She realized he had a box of donuts in his other hand.

"I wanted to be here in time to take you to church," he admitted, "but I thought maybe I should bring breakfast, too."

She laughed, a melodic sound Brad loved hearing. "I just finished making coffee and was trying to figure out what I wanted to eat. Come on in."

Leaving the door open she went back to the kitchen. Brad followed. Dani took out another cup and poured coffee. The two of them sat at the table to dig into the sugary delights in the box.

After a jelly filled bismark, Dani excused herself to go finish dressing. In less than ten minutes she returned ready to go. They drove to the church. Dani knew her being there would cause a stir among the town's people. She had not attended regularly since moving back. Being there with Brad would give every mother of a single girl something to talk about, too. Dani had not forgotten how small towns worked. Today, she was not going to let anything spoil it.

Hand-in-hand Brad and Dani walked into the church. They greeted old friends; Brad introduced her to some new people in town. Then they found seats about midway down the aisle. The service was pleasant. Dani did not know this minister well. He had presided over her grandmother's funeral a few months earlier and done a nice job.

While not deeply religious, Dani always found the old hymns and the scriptures comforting. They seemed to appeal to her on an inner level she could never explain in words.

After church, they stayed for coffee and to talk with friends. It was the first time Dani had seen many of them since her grand-mother's passing. A few had word of sympathy to offer. Dani knew her grandmother had been well liked in the community. Someone in the group asked if Dani was staying and she assured them she was. After about the third time Brad heard her answer she was staying he put his arm around her shoulder and said with a smile, "I'm doing my best to convince her it's in her best interests to stay."

The woman Dani had been talking to replied, "I hope you are not the only reason she would stay." Then she turned and walked away.

Dani stifled a chuckle.

"Not funny," he told her.

"Oh, yes, it is."

They left shortly after and made their way back to Dani's. She was surprised to see his overnight bag in the back seat.

"Are you planning to work today?" she inquired.

"Unless you have something else planned, I was."

"No, it's fine with me."

They drove back in comfortable silence. As they went inside, Brad asked, "Do you have someplace I can change?"

"Sure, pick any bedroom," she answered.

"Thanks." Brad went up and picked the first bedroom. He had not realized Dani was using her old room. He changed quickly and made his way back downstairs.

He found her in her office. "What time is dinner? I'll need to change back into my dress clothes."

Dani let out a belly laugh bringing tears to her eyes. "Honestly," she began when she could talk again, "we no longer do formal Sunday dinners. But Ella told me two hours."

"Okay, I'm off to work. If I don't come back in two hours you know where to find me." He turned and headed for the linen closet and the secret chamber.

Brad made a discovery that afternoon, one Dani had made as a child. The sounds from the rooms the other side of the tunnel walls carried through. A voice he was not familiar with was saying, "I heard it again. I know there's a ghost here, just listen."

To which Ella replied, "Child, this is an old house. Old houses make noise. I've been here for forty years and there are no ghosts; now get to your chores."

Brad chuckled and went to work putting in the rest of the insulation and the sound proofing board so; he could start the dry wall tomorrow night. He would bet his next paycheck Dani had added her own spooky noises to keep staff wondering. The idea kept him smiling for quite a while as he worked.

He made his way upstairs and into the bathroom to wash up without being seen, then headed toward Dani's office. He was not sure what she was studying, but he knew it's where she would be.

Dani had been reading and making notes while Brad worked. She had just finished her proposal and it was coming off her printer as he entered. She glanced up and said, "One minute and I'll be done."

Brad nodded affirmatively and waited.

Ella had gone all out for Sunday dinner. Salad, vegetables, mashed potatoes, gravy, baked chicken, rolls, and something hidden under the dessert cover. Brad decided with this feast he was done working for the day. He and Dani served themselves and Ella left to go home to dinner with Sam. Dani sent the new girl home, too.

"Are we alone now?" Brad asked and Dani could see the mischief in his eyes.

"Yes, should I be worried?"

"No, but I learned one of your secrets today," he told her.

"I have no secrets," she insisted.

"Oh, but you do," he leaned in conspiratorially and whispered, "I know some of the servants think this house is haunted. There was a young girl who lived here and eaves dropped on conversations. I'm willing to wager she also added to the belief in ghosts by adding her own sounds." He sat back and began to eat his dinner.

"Did you find my old chains?" she asked with a bit of devilry.

"No, I overheard your new girl complaining about ghosts."

"I sure hope you added a few ghostly sounds," Dani said in all seriousness. "I think Ella and I are going to have to find someone new to train. The girl sneaks into rooms and then acts like she's done something wrong when you find her there. Not to mention she's afraid of her own shadow."

"You think ghostly sounds might make her quit on her own?" Brad asked.

"I would hope so," she answered and speared a piece of broccoli.

Brad chuckled as he thought about it. He knew first-hand how it felt to fire someone. He did not envy Dani the task. On the other hand, he had never considered scaring an employee into quitting.

"Do you want to see how it looks so far?" he asked.

Standing Dani said, "Lead the way."

Together they headed into the closet and the secret tunnel. Dani liked the subtle but consistent lighting leading the way to the chamber room. The room no longer had an abandoned look to it. It even felt warmer.

"I put the insulation in then added sound proofing. No one can hear us now and we can no longer hear anyone else. Next will come the drywall. Once it's up, you can help with the paint brush," he told her with a chuckle.

"Be glad to help," she told him.

"I'll be putting in a sink, toilet, and shower. I even allowed for a second sink in this room to do dishes. The plug for the small fridge is in and you can use an electric frying pan as well as a microwave down here. I even have a place for a small TV," he showed her with his hands.

"You have been busy," she agreed.

"Want to walk by the river?" he asked not knowing what else she needed to know right now.

"Oh, yes," she said softly.

Heading out the tunnel they made their way to the river bank. Dani walked to the end of the dock and sat down, took her shoes off, and hung her feet into the river. Brad joined her and they sat in companionable silence for a while. Finally breaking the silence he asked, "Do we need to talk about the future?"

Looking at him in the early dusk, Dani said, "If you think we should."

Brad took her shoulders and turned her so she was facing him. "I love you. I want you to be my wife. To spend my life showing you how much you mean to me. Tell me what I have to do to make that happen."

"I don't know," she answered him with honesty. "I love you. I have since we were kids. You just left, I don't want to wake up some morning and find you gone again."

He pulled her to him and kissed her. When the kiss broke he told her, "I messed up a long time ago. I'm not going anywhere this time."

"I want to believe you," she said. "I'm just afraid. I cannot go through the hurt of losing you a second time. I think it would crush me beyond repair."

"Then we'll work on it," he assured her. "I am in no rush."

She leaned into him saying nothing.

CHAPTER NINE

Dani was up early and had breakfast ready for Brad when he arrived. They talked briefly then Dani excused herself. She had much to do this morning. Maureen would be here and she would be officially open for business today.

When Maureen arrived, Dani was already at her desk. She had scoured the morning paper to see what might be coming up for trial. Her briefcase was ready and she had only to put on her jacket for her first appearance in court. She was going to sit all day in the hopes a judge would assign a case to her. Maureen did an inventory of what supplies were already there and made a short list of things she knew would be needed.

She knocked on Dani's door before entering. Dani looked up and smiled. "You need not knock if my door is open, Maureen. It's a formality not needed in an office this small."

"As you wish," Maureen replied. "I made a list of the things still needed in the office. Where would you like them purchased?"

"Isn't there a local office supply store?" Dani inquired.

"Oh, yes, Willowbees' and they deliver," Maureen said quickly. "Shall I set up an account there?"

"By all means, I like buying local and the delivery is a bonus."

Maureen turned saying, "I'll get right on it and we should have these items by tomorrow."

"Thank you," Dani responded as she stood to put on her jacket. "I'll be at the court house until at least lunch time. If I haven't snagged a case by then, I'll call you, get a message, check and let you know how the afternoon will look. I think Mr. Wilkins is coming in tomorrow morning to go over his will."

"I'll double check with him. Have a smashing day, Miss Dani," Maureen said as Dani swept through the door on her way out.

Maureen's first task for the day was to label the file cabinets for case files and accounting files. She had finished the case file cabinet when Ella showed up.

"I'm sorry to bother you, but I generally bring Miss Dani something to drink and a snack about this time of day," Ella said quietly. "I brought you some sweet tea and a snack."

Flattered beyond belief, Maureen replied, "I thank you. I didn't expect this. I'm Maureen Beckett." She held her hand out to Ella, who took it warmly.

"I'm, Ella, the head housekeeper. If you need anything Mrs. Beckett, you just let me know."

"Only if you call me, Maureen," she replied smiling. "And sometimes will you consider joining me in a snack or lunch?"

"You would be most welcome to come to the kitchen for lunch," Ella said with pride. "I'll send Chloe for you when it's ready, Maureen."

"Wonderful," Maureen started, to be interrupted by the ringing phone. She reached for the phone as Ella silently left the room. "Montgomery Law Office, how may I help you?" she said into the phone as she reached for a pen and her note pad.

"This is Detective Macy McVannel of the Rivers Edge Police Department, may I speak with Ms. Montgomery, please."

"I'm sorry, Detective McVannel, Ms. Montgomery is in court this morning. I can schedule you an appointment or have her return your call this afternoon," Maureen replied.

"Would you ask her to call me, please?" Macy responded giving her cell number for Dani to call. "Thank you."

"I'll have her call you as soon as she calls in for her messages," Maureen assured her then hung up the phone. She wondered why a detective from a neighboring town would be calling Dani. Oh well, not her business. Maureen ate the snack Ella had left and went to work on the accounting file cabinet.

The phone range just as Chloe came to tell her lunch was ready. Maureen reached for the phone while putting up a finger for Chloe to wait. "Montgomery Law Office, how may I help you?"

"Maureen, it's Dani. Were there any calls?"

"Yes, a Detective McVannel from Rivers Edge called," Maureen replied. "She left her number and asked you to call her at your earliest convenience." Maureen read the number to Dani and awaited further instructions.

"Great I'll call her on my way back," Dani replied. "I should be there in about half an hour."

"I'll see you then," Maureen replied hanging up the phone she rose to follow Chloe to the kitchen.

DANI DIALED THE number Macy had given as she walked to her car.

"McVannel," Macy said answering.

"Macy, it's Dani. Maureen said you called."

"Hi, Dani, I did," was Macy's cheery reply. "I'd like to set a time to meet with you. I have a case I need to pick your brain on and it would be good to do some catching up."

Dani had reached her car. "Let me get into my car and I'll look at my calendar."

Macy waited the minute or two it took Dani to get into her car and lock her doors. "Okay, I have my planner," Dani said. "How does Thursday work for you? I can meet you for lunch and clear my afternoon."

"If it's okay with you, I'll come to your office," Macy replied. "I want to talk case then we can go get lunch and catch up."

"Sounds like a plan, I've put you in for one o'clock," Dani told her.

"I'll be there," Macy said and disconnected.

Dani took a moment to wonder what was going on, then started her car and headed for home. There had been nothing on the court docket for the afternoon and she had not been assigned a case this morning. It would give her time to research her venture rescuing battered women.

CHAPTER TEN

Maureen was returning to the office when Dani came in. "Did you get any assignments?" she asked.

"Not today and the docket was empty this afternoon," Dani replied. "I'm going to grab some lunch from the kitchen. You did eat didn't you?"

"Yes, Ella came and invited me to have lunch in the kitchen."

"Wonderful," Dani said smiling. "Now I get to convince her I'm starving." Laughing she headed for the kitchen.

Maureen did not think Dani would have any problem convincing Ella to feed her. Ella practically doted on her. Maureen was feeling pretty lucky to have found this job.

ELLA FUSSED AT Dani for not having lunch in town, but she made something for her to eat. Dani picked up the plate and said, "Thanks, Ella, you're the best. I'm going to eat at my desk."

"Perfectly good kitchen and she's going to eat at her desk," Ella muttered.

Dani stifled a giggle and walked toward her office. Working at home was going to have its perks; lunch would be one of them. She stopped at Maureen's desk.

"I have an appointment at one on Thursday with Detective McVannel," she stated. "Please keep my afternoon free."

"I sure will," Maureen responded putting the information on her desk calendar and turning to the computer to put it in there. "Is there anything you need from me right now?"

"No, thank you. I'm going to eat and do some research," Dani replied. She went to her desk booted up her computer and began eating her lunch.

Maureen's phone rang a couple more times before the end of the day. She spoke with each person and scheduled them afternoon appointments for the next day. She cleared her desk and went to say goodnight to Dani.

"Miss Dani," she started entering Dani's office, "oh, I'm so sorry."

"It's alright, Maureen," Dani assured her as she dried her eyes and set down the photo she'd been looking at as she cried. "Please come in and close the door. I need to talk to you about something."

Maureen shut the door and took a seat in front of Dani, "Have I offended you in anyway?"

"Heaven's no," Dani said with a chuckle. "I am taking on a project and I want you to know about it. If you choose not to work for me, I will understand and will pay you through the end of the week."

Maureen relaxed a bit still not sure what she had walked into. Dani Montgomery had seemed so together when they had interviewed. She believed she had found a job to take her to retirement.

Dani took a deep breath, "I'm not sure how to tell you this. I've been doing research on a modern day underground railroad. This project helps abused women and their children escape and start over new. They are provided with identity, seed money, and job training where necessary. My part in this will be to provide them sanctuary on the way to their new home."

"Oh my, what a wonderful thing you are doing," Maureen said relieved.

"I was hoping you would think so," the relief in Dani's voice was palpable. "I was afraid you might not want to work with me. Doing this is questionable in the legal world. It's not illegal, but I'm not sure it is legal either. I might know more after I speak with Detective McVannel."

Maureen visibly straightened in her seat, "I don't care how legal it is or not, it is something we should do."

"Glad you are on board with it," Dani assured her. "I will do my best to keep you on the outer reaches of this. For now will you take a walk with me? I know you are ready to go home and I won't keep you long."

Standing Maureen indicated she was willing. The two went out the front door and walked around the house toward the river.

"I used to play here as a child," Dani told her. "On one of my many explorations I found this." Dani led the way toward a brushy area.

Maureen followed and was stunned when they came upon a door. Dani produced a key and unlocked the door. Stepping in she flipped a switch and soft light came on. Maureen could see light for quite a distance down what looked to be a cave tunnel. She continued to follow Dani. Suddenly the room widened and she could see someone had been busy working on the room.

"This is where the women and children will stay," Dani told her. "No one on my staff knows this is here."

"But someone has been busy working down here," Maureen observed. "I see the electrical, drywall, insulation, and tools."

"Yes," Dani chuckled. "I have coerced someone into helping me. It is better you not know who."

"I understand," Maureen said nodding as she looked around. "Where do the stairs lead?"

"They lead to the main house," Dani told her. "We will go out through there as I locked the cave door when we came in."

"Sounds good," Maureen assured her. "When do we start housing people?"

Dani was thoughtful before answering, "I don't know yet. I am still building connections with the network. There is at least six weeks of work left to do here. I want you to be sure you are okay with this."

"I am more than okay with this," Maureen's voice was filled with excitement. "Tell me what you need from me. I am only too happy to help."

"As we get nearer to completion, I will let you know," Dani beamed with delight, "this way to home."

The two women made their way into the linen closet and down to the office without being seen. Maureen collected her purse and let herself out. Dani returned to her office and finished her presentation for Macy.

CHAPTER ELEVEN

uesday was nothing special in Dani's life. She spent the morning in court hoping for a case with no luck. Her afternoon she spoke with two people about wills and trusts. She took on both and went to work on each as soon as the person had left. Completing the first one before the second person arrived. Maureen was fitting in with the house staff and proving to be a valuable asset to Dani, answering the phone, scheduling clients, and keeping things running smoothly. Often Dani would ask her into her office when Ella brought the morning snack. They were settling into a good routine.

Dani liked the routine. Brad still came for dinner and to work on the secret chamber. Last night she had gone down with him to hold up the drywall while he installed it. Finally she could see it coming together. She wanted bright cheery colors in the room and hallways. Since her guests would not be outside, she wanted to be sure they didn't feel as though they were in prison. She was also thinking about games and things for children. Something they could take with them or leave behind. Dani was not sure yet.

Dani also found time to contact someone who was working in the rescue program. They would be meeting in the near future to begin making plans for Dani's first visitors. She was excited and apprehensive at the same time. Excited to be doing something worthwhile, apprehensive about what it might mean from a legal standpoint. As soon as she knew for sure she would talk to Brad, Macy, and Maureen. There would be no turning back once they started.

OUT OF THE house and heading for the courthouse, Dani was thinking about her meeting with Macy in two days. Macy wanted to talk work before lunch. She wanted lunch before approaching Macy with her idea to rescue the down trodden. Either way it would be a win. It had been a while since she and Macy had spent time together.

In the court house, Dani took a seat midway down the aisle. She was hoping maybe there would be a case for her today. The bailiff asked them to rise as the judge entered. She had not seen today's docket, so was not sure what was there. Several people sat waiting for the judge to begin, some must have been family members of the accused or victims, and others appeared to be attorneys. It would be interesting.

"Bailiff, call our first case," the judge said.

"Windham County vs. Theodore S. Jackman, Mr. Jackman is accused of beating his wife Eliza. Mrs. Jackman is currently in the hospital recovering from her injuries," stated the bailiff in a voice devoid of emotion.

Mr. Jackman had been sitting along a wall of people to be arraigned. He was escorted to the defense table. No one stood to represent him. Dani held her breath.

The prosecutor was seated at his table. He did not blink, just sat patiently.

"Mr. Jackman," the judge began, "are you able to afford an attorney?"

"No, sir," Jackman replied.

The judge looked around the courtroom. "I see Miss Montgomery here today. Would you come forward to represent Mr. Jackman, please?"

Dani let out the breath she had been holding and stood. Slowly she approached the defense table. She looked at the judge and asked, "Your Honor, may I have a moment to confer with my client?"

"You have five minutes, make it happen," the judge told her.

She looked at Mr. Jackman and whispered, "I don't want to hear your story right this minute, just plead not guilty. Do you have any money for bail?"

He shook his head no while looking at a spot above her head.

"Okay, I'll see what I can do on it," she assured him. Then looking at the judge she said, "We are ready to proceed, Your Honor."

The judge turned to the prosecution, "Mr. Stamm, begin."

Richard Stamm stood and began, "The people are charging Mr. Jackman with battery and attempted murder. We seek remand."

"How does the defendant plead," the judge asked.

Jackman looked at him and quietly said, "Not guilty, sir."

"Counselor, on bail?" the judge asked.

"We are seeking some kind of bond Your Honor, Mrs. Jackman is safe in the hospital at this time," Dani responded. She hated not knowing anything about the situation.

Stamm spoke up immediately, "Mr. Jackman is a repeat offender. He has spent time in jail for assault previously."

"Is this true, Mr. Jackman?" the judge asked.

"Yes, sir, for a barroom brawl," Jackman answered.

"Remand," the judge said banging his gavel. "Next case."

Dani whispered, "I'll talk with you in a few minutes." Then Mr. Jackman was led away.

Dani left the court room in search of a conference room to use. Finding one across from the courtroom, she motioned to the guard to bring Mr. Jackman there. He complied.

Inside the conference room Jackman was seated. The guard stepped outside to give them privacy and to prevent the man from escaping. Jackman seated himself in a chair hands still cuffed in front of him.

Dani began, "Mr. Jackman, I am Danielle Montgomery and will be your attorney. At any time you feel I am not giving you adequate representation you may ask the judge to replace me. Do you understand?"

Theodore Jackman looked at her before asking, "Are you any good?"

"I've won my fair share of cases, I've lost a few, too," she responded. "Anything you say to me is confidential. Since I've not read the police report, please tell me what happened."

He shook his head of shaggy brown hair and replied, "I don't honestly know. I remember drinking after work. I remember Lizzy coming to get me, but I am blank until the ambulance arrived and they arrested me."

"Have you hit your wife before?" Dani asked.

"Sure, I've smacked her a couple of times," he admitted. "I like my woman to know who's boss."

"Do you have children?" Dani asked.

"Yeah, we got two," he answered. "Her folks probably have them now."

"What about this barroom brawl?" she asked.

"We were drinking at the Watering Hole and some fella got lippy. He took a swing at me and I swung back," he paused. "We both done thirty days in the lock up. No big deal."

"It will be a big deal if we go to trial," she assured him. "Let me get on this, read the police report, talk to your wife, and the neighbors then see where we should go. I should be back with you late tomorrow or Friday."

He looked at her again, his brown eyes taking in all of her, "Whatever you say."

She knocked on the door and the guard entered and took Jackman away. Dani shook her head. Not the kind of case she had hoped for, but maybe the first candidate for sanctuary. She went in search of case records so she could head home to start on the case. First she got police reports on this incident and the barroom brawl Jackman had admitted to being in. She then asked for the 9-1-1 recording of the call for the most recent incident. Finally she headed to the hospital to see how Mrs. Jackman was doing.

At the hospital the nurses were reluctant to let her see Mrs. Jackman, but Dani won them over when she said she detested wife beaters. They told her which room and Dani walked down the hallway.

Lizzy Jackman looked tiny and fragile lying in the hospital bed. Her blonde hair lay around her head as she gazed out the window. She was a fair woman which made her bruises stand out. She had a black eye and a small cut above the other, her lip was split and held together by a butterfly bandage. It was the cast on her left arm which made Dani catch her breath. She was unable to tell if there were any other injuries. She knocked softly on the door. Lizzy turned to look at her and said, "Do come in."

"I'm Dani Montgomery, Mrs. Jackman," she began.

"Oh the lawyer who is defending Ted," Lizzy commented.

"Yes, I'd like to ask you some questions if I may," Dani asked smiling.

Lizzy looked at her for a moment then asked, "How can you defend a man who beats his wife?"

"To be honest, I usually don't," Dani told her. "I was assigned to your husband by the court. I have talked to him and he tells me he doesn't remember what happened."

"Sounds like Ted," she scoffed. "I expect him here anytime carryin' a bouquet of flowers and being all sweet sayin' he's sorry."

"I take it this has happened before," Dani stated.

"Ever since my son was born eight years ago," Lizzy confirmed. "This is the first time the cops have been called. Usually he just drops me off after at an urgent care. They patch me up and send me home."

"Has he ever hurt your children?" Dani asked.

"No, I always step between him and the kids," she said resignedly. "Who is watchin' them do you know?"

Dani seemed shocked she did not know where her children were. "I don't, but I will check with family services. Do you have family who could take them in?"

Lizzy shook her head slightly to indicate she did not. "My folks been gone for years, I got no family, but my kids."

"I'll find them. Then I'm going to bring you papers to sign so they can stay with me until you are well enough to go home," Dani told her. "You are to rest as long as you need to. I'll arrange for your bill to be handled."

"Why are you doin' this for me?" Lizzy asked.

"Someday I'll tell you, but for now I need to make sure your husband takes a plea deal," Dani told her. "He won't be able to do this to you again."

"Once he's out, he'll come back," Lizzy assured her.

"Maybe you won't be here waiting for him," suggested Dani.

"Got nowhere to go," Lizzy confirmed.

"You, let me worry about where you might go," Dani told her patting her good arm. "I'll be back tomorrow and you can tell me what happened. Rest now."

"Thank you," Lizzy said as Dani left the room.

Dani was on a mission to find Lizzy's kids. As soon as she stepped out of the hospital she called Maureen.

"Montgomery Law Office, how may I help you?" Maureen said as she answered the phone.

"Maureen, it's Dani, I need you to find out where the Jackman children were taken when their father was arrested last night. Mother is Elizabeth Jackman and is in Windham General. Father is still in jail."

"I'm on it Miss Dani," Maureen assured her and hung up the phone to begin making calls. She would have the answer when Miss Dani arrived.

Dani headed to her car to make her way to the office. She knew Maureen would have the information as soon as she could. It was time to tackle this case and get ready for preliminary trial. Hopefully the DA-District Attorney-would go for a deal. It would be the best outcome all around. It would buy Dani time to help Lizzy and the kids relocate.

CHAPTER TWELVE

Dani arrived back at her home office about twenty minutes later. She put coffee on and took out a clean note pad. "Miss Dani," Maureen started as she entered Dani's office. "I found the Jackman children. Children's Services placed them in Willow Dale Center." She made a face as she said it.

"Tell me about Willow Dale Center," Dani said softly.

"They usually only place juvenile offenders there until they are arraigned," Maureen said. "The shelters and foster homes must have been filled."

"Okay, get a guardianship paper drawn up," Dani began. "I will be taking custody of the children before the end of the day. Can you run up to the hospital and get Lizzy Jackman's signature? Have a couple nurses witness it and take it to children's court?"

"Sure thing," Maureen said heading for her desk.

"I need you to stay in children's court until the judge signs it and then pick up the children from that awful place," Dani continued. "They will be staying here until their mother is ready to come home from the hospital."

Maureen looked at Dani, not sure if she had lost her mind or grown angel wings, "I'm on it." She turned and began the work she needed to do.

Dani headed to the kitchen to find Ella. She was going to need to know about the two unexpected visitors they were going to have. She needed two bedrooms readied and there would be two extras at dinner.

She was returning to her office when Macy arrived. The two women hugged and Dani led her in closing the door behind them.

"I'm so glad to see you, but you are two days early," Dani said as she poured coffee for herself and tea for Macy.

Macy took the cup, "Thanks, I couldn't wait. Hope it's not a problem."

"No at all, I didn't pick up my first case until this morning," Dani assured her. "So, what is the business you need to see me about?"

"Buckle up this is a bad one," Macy told her. "I got a case last fall which made my skin crawl. We were called to the ADA's (Assistant District Attorney) office. There we encountered a woman whose sixteen year old daughter had attempted suicide. Turns out someone took a photo of her in the locker room shower and plastered it all over cyberspace and sent it to cell phones." She stopped to sip her tea.

"There's more?" Dani asked.

"Much, but the thing bugging me is the defendant had a nervous breakdown at age twelve and we cannot get records," Macy admitted. "So, when she broke down in court, the trial had to be postponed. Justice hasn't been served."

Dani took her time, then asked, "What you want from me is to find the records?"

"If you think you can," Macy stated. She leaned back in the chair gauging Dani's reaction.

"It shouldn't be too difficult," Dani assured her. "I will get on it first thing tomorrow."

"I'm so glad you can do this," Macy said relieved. "It has haunted me."

"How did this case get to you?" Dani wanted to know.

"Kids hurting kids, is wrong on all levels," Macy began. "The girl accused of being the mastermind of all this, really got under my skin. She has no idea her actions have had serious consequences. Not to mention she is annoying."

"Ouch," Dani commented. "You rarely let people get to you. How are you coping?"

"Eli, my partner, Tom Maxwell, some of the other officers both county and state, and I have started volunteering at the local high school on our days off. Bullying has pretty much come to a halt and the kids are opening to us when they do encounter bullying. We sit with both parties to see if we can figure out the cause. Sometimes, bullies just want attention. Other times it's just because they can. Still others are victims of bullies at home," she told Dani.

"Wow, I'm impressed," Dani said and clearly she was. "This is your save the world campaign one kid at a time, right?"

Macy laughed and Dani could see the tension leaving her friend, "I hadn't thought of it as such, but maybe it is."

Smiling Dani took their cups to the sink and asked, "So, where do you want to go for lunch? We need some serious girl time."

"Oh, yes we do," Macy agreed. "I don't care where we eat as long as we can just talk like old times."

"Sounds like a plan," Dani said. "Maureen set the phone to the answering machine. I have her on an errand. There is no need for me to be home before dinner. Let's get out of here."

The two women laughed and walked arm-in-arm to the door. Dani closed up the office and they took Macy's car to find a late lunch.

OVER SALADS THE women caught up on the men in their lives. Dani started by saying, "You didn't tell me Eli owned the Log Cabin Inn."

Macy tossed her head as she laughed, "It's a hobby according to him. Although, he did say something about leaving the force to cook full time."

"Wow, he'd do that for you?" Dani put down her fork and looked at her friend. "Would he be happy with not being a police officer?"

"I have no idea," Macy told her. "I'm not letting him quit."

"Now you sound like the Macy I know," Dani smiled as she responded.

"He is a good man," Macy began. "In fact, he's everything I could ever want in a man. I just have to get over my fear of losing him."

Dani paused before saying, "You know he might have the same fear."

It took Macy a minute to digest what her friend had just said. Then she replied, "I never thought of him worrying about me."

It was Dani's turn to be shocked. She concentrated on her salad. Leaving Macy to give it more thought.

Macy ate a bit then said, "Spill it about you and Brad. I thought you'd excised him for sure."

Being mid swallow Dani finished her bite then answered, "I never got over him. I moved home to be near him. Funny he bought property across the river from the Willows to be able to see me. I still love him, Macy."

"Hmm, and how does Mr. Wonderful feel about you?" Macy asked with heavy sarcasm.

"Surprisingly, he loves me," Dani answered. "He's gone out of his way to be the perfect gentleman and to show me how much he still cares." She nibbled on her salad before continuing, "He never married, because he was waiting for me."

"So he says," Macy scoffed. "I remember the first two years of college. You wouldn't even look at another guy. I could hardly believe it the night you told us you had a date."

"People change," Dani defended. "We were young, too young for the feelings we had. We're older now."

"I hope you don't get hurt again," Macy told her.

Dani smiled, "I'm so glad you care."

They finished lunch, did some shopping, and on the way back to Dani's she broached the topic nearest to her heart. "Macy, I have a new project. I'd like you to be a part of it."

"What have you got in mind? Macy asked turning to watch her friend.

"I need to show you something at the house," Dani told her, "then I'll explain everything. I have a written proposal for you to take home and read."

"This must be some serious project for you to have written a proposal," Macy said. "Are you sure?"

"Very sure, I've got two other people who are interested in helping me," Dani assured her. "I have not given them the proposal yet, I wanted you to be first."

"So, can I get a preview before we arrive?" Macy asked.

"No, it's something I have to show you," Dani replied.

The two remained silent for the rest of the trip. Once at Dani's they got out of the car, leaving their packages in it. Dani led the way to the river.

"Okay, so I've been to this spot with you a million times, Dani," Macy said with exasperation. "What makes it so special?"

Dani walked toward a bushy area, "This." She led the way to the cave door and put a key in the lock. They walked inside Dani flipped a switch allowing the lights in the tunnel to flicker on.

"Where does this lead?" Macy asked.

"Follow me," Dani said leading the way to the chamber room.

"Holy smokes," Macy said looking around. She saw where the toilet, shower, and sink had been installed. There was new flooring in the bathroom.

"I don't understand, where are we and what are you building?"

"I'm building a sanctuary," Dani said simply. "The tunnel over there," she said pointing to her right, "leads to a linen closet in my house. I discovered this place as a kid."

"You had a secret hideaway and never said a word," Macy's voice was excited in spite of her being awed.

Dani smiled. "Are you going to ask me who gets sanctuary?"

"I'll bite. Who?"

"Any woman who needs to escape an abusive partner," Dani told her. "I'm even going to allow them to bring their kids."

Macy stared at Dani, "Is this even legal?"

"It's the reason I drew up a proposal," Dani stated. "I don't exactly know. I've been in touch with a group who does this and I hope to be part of the network in about six weeks."

Macy shook her head in wonder, "This is to make up for Michelle, isn't it?"

"Partly," Dani admitted. "A part of me is doing this because it's the right thing."

"Let's go get this proposal," Macy said. "I'm having dinner with Eli tonight. Do we need a contract or something for you to look into Chelsie Patton for me?"

"You mean like a retainer?" Dani asked. "No, I'll bill you if I find something." She led the way to the linen closet. The two of them went out the front door just as Maureen was arriving with two young children.

"Miss Dani, I'd like you to meet, Teddy and Amy Jackman," Maureen said. She turned to Teddy and Amy saying, "This is the nice lady who is going to let you stay with her until your mom gets better."

Teddy looked at Dani before putting out his hand to shake hers, "Are you going to keep my dad from hurting my mom?"

"I hope to, Teddy," she assured him. She turned to Macy. This is my friend Detective McVannel, she will help me."

Teddy held out his hand for Macy to shake, "Nice to meet you."

"The pleasure is all mine, Teddy," she told him. Then she leaned down to speak to Amy, "Miss Dani will take very good care of you."

Amy just nodded to show she understood.

Macy made her way to the car and retrieved Dani's packages, handed them to her, took one last look at her friend and new charges, then got into her car and drove home. She wondered about the two children and Dani's project. *Maybe it would be a good idea to have Eli go over the proposal with her.*

CHAPTER THIRTEEN

ani took the two children inside. She thanked Maureen and sent her home. Upstairs she put them in the old nursery. It had two beds in it. Dani had not made any changes to the room yet.

"You can stay here," she told them. "Tomorrow I have to talk to your dad, then I'll pick up some toys for you to play with. Is there anything special you'd like?"

"I like cars and trucks," Teddy told her. "Amy likes to color."

"There are sure to be some cars and trucks with me when I come home," Dani assured him. Turning to Amy she said, "What do you like to color?"

Amy who was a tiny version of her mom said in a soft voice, "Butterflies and fairies."

"Oh, those are my favorite," Dani exclaimed. "Do either of you like books or games?"

"We don't have any books and we don't know how to play games," Teddy told her. "My dad says they just get in the way."

"I'll tell you what," Dani said, "I'm declaring tomorrow night game night and every Wednesday you are here we will have game night. I'll see if I can find some simple games."

Amy's eyes seemed to grow in size, "Are you sure we won't get into trouble?"

Dani reached for the little girl, "I'm sure. How about you two go right in there to the bathroom and wash up for dinner? I have some company coming and I need to take care of some packages.

"Okay, Miss Dani," Teddy said taking his sister's hand and leading her into the bathroom.

Dani went down to get her packages, glad she had picked up a couple of bedtime stories. Brad pulled in as she was heading to the door so, she stopped and waited for him.

He pulled her into his arms for a kiss, not minding the packages she held. "How was your day?" he asked letting her go.

"Very interesting, we have a couple of guests for dinner," she told him. "They are going to be with me for a while."

"Guests, I should have dressed up?" he questioned smiling.

"I don't think they'll care," she assured him leading the way into the house. "Let me take these upstairs, I'll bring my guests down and meet you in the dining room."

Brad seemed baffled as he had not seen another car in the driveway, "Sure, okay." He turned and headed for the dining room. The aroma of home cooked dinner making his mouth water. He had barely had time to enter when he turned at the sound of children behind him. Stunned he watched Dani enter with a young man on one side of her and a little girl holding her other hand. Dani was smiling as she listened intently to the little boy.

She looked up to find Brad staring at her. She chuckled at the expression on his face. "Brad, I'd like you to meet Teddy and Amy Jackman, they will be staying with me for a few days," she said by way of explanation.

Teddy stepped forward and held out his hand to shake Brad's while saying, "Nice to meet you, sir."

"Nice to meet you, too, Teddy," Brad told him taking his hand. "You may call me Brad." He turned to Amy, "Hello, there Sunshine, how are you?"

Amy clung to Dani, but softly answered, "I'm fine, thank you."

"Let's have dinner," Dani said leading the way to the table. She sat Teddy on one side of her and Amy on the other. Brad sat across from Dani. Ella brought the main course and served everyone.

"Miss Dani, will you be needing anything else," she asked.

"No, Ella, you go home and enjoy your evening with Sam," Dani assured her. "I'll load the dishwasher when we're done."

Nodding Ella left. For the first time ever she was not muttering as she left.

Brad asked, "Is Ella sick?"

Dani looked at him and replied, "I am not aware she is. Why do you ask?"

Laughing he answered, "She didn't do her usual muttering as she left."

Dani let out a hardy laugh, when she caught her breath saying, "I'm sure it has to do with the household changes and she's still in shock."

Turning to Teddy, Brad asked, "What types of things are you interested in?"

Smiling because he was being included in the conversation, Teddy answered, "I'm interested in lots of things, but I don't get to do too many."

"Well, what's the one thing you'd most like to do?" Brad asked.

"I'd like to learn to play baseball," was Teddy's quick response.

"Maybe I could come by on Saturday and teach you," Brad offered. "We could include Amy if she's interested."

Amy shrank hearing her name. She turned big blue eyes on Brad, "I'd rather get my nails painted, if it's alright?"

"I'm sure Miss Dani could find a way to fit it into her schedule," Brad suggested winking at Dani.

Picking up on the hint Dani replied, "I think Amy and I will spend the morning becoming glamorous. Maybe the two of you will join us by the river for a picnic in the afternoon?"

Teddy was first to answer, "A real picnic? I'd love it."

"Then after we hang out and teach you some baseball, we'll get cleaned up and meet the ladies by the river," Brad told him. He looked an Amy and Dani, "It's a date ladies."

They finished dinner and Dani took the children to the parlor. "Do you want to watch TV or listen to me read a book?" she asked.

The children looked at each other, then Teddy asked, "You would read to us?"

"Sure, let's get you ready for bed first," Dani suggested. "I bought a few books today. We can read one or start one and read some each night."

"I love books," Amy said, her soft voice filling the room.

They headed upstairs to get changed. Once they came back down, they settled on either side of Dani on the sofa. She had a bag at her feet.

"We didn't do game night tonight, but I think we can squeeze it in tomorrow if it's okay with you," Dani told them.

"Sure tomorrow is good," Teddy told her with the air of someone who is used to disappointment.

She leaned down and pulled the bag onto her lap, "Well, I did some shopping before I knew anything about you. Teddy, I hope this set of cars will be a good start," she handed him a box of matchbox cars and trucks.

"Oh, wow, thank you," he exclaimed. He looked the box over then asked, "Is it okay to open them?"

"Sure," Dani told him reaching into the bag again. "Amy, I bought some coloring books and crayons, but I remembered liking paper dolls when I was younger." She took the coloring books, crayons, and packets of paper dolls and set them on Amy's lap.

"Miss Dani, I don't know what a paper doll is," Amy's eyes brimmed with tears at this revelation.

"It's okay, Pumpkin, I'll show you."

Teddy was on the floor with his cars and trucks, so Dani opened one of the paper doll packets. It was of all the Disney princesses. She showed Amy how to take out the dolls, and cut out a few outfits so Amy could try them on her dolls.

An hour later all toys put away, the children were back on the sofa with Dani. She opened a book she had purchased and began reading, *Jungle Book* by Rudyard Kipling.

Teddy laughed, "Who would name a kid Rudyard?"

"Good question, Teddy," Dani answered, "I suspect it was probably a family name. Like his mom's name before she got married."

The story began and Dani closed the book when she realized both children were sound asleep. Brad found her between the kids when he came in. He carried Teddy up the stairs and Dani carried Amy, "In the nursery on the left," she whispered. They placed the children in bed, tucked them in, and left with a night light burning.

"You are good with them," Brad told her as they made their way to her office. "What's their story?"

Dani made her way to the bar and fixed drinks, handing Brad his she told him about being assigned to their father's case. She then told him about visiting their mother and learning the children had been housed in a juvenile detention center.

"So, I'm going to keep them until she's well enough to go home," Dani concluded.

"How are you going to be able to defend their father?" Brad asked.

"I'm not sure yet," she conceded. "After I go over all the discovery material and his past record, I'll meet with the district attorney and see how he wants to proceed."

"Don't get too attached to them," Brad said nodding his head toward the stairs. "They do have to go home."

"I know," she told him. "I am worried this might be my first group for escape. It will depend on the prosecution."

Brad took a drink and said nothing. He was still not convinced Dani's project was viable.

She reached into her desk and pulled out a file. Handing it to him she said, "I know you have misgivings. Please, take this home and read it. I have worked hard on this proposal. I gave one to Macy today after lunch and I have one for my secretary, Maureen."

Brad took the file. "Dani, I'm going to help you even if I'm not sure how it works. I believe in you." He took his glass to the bar. "I really need to get home."

She rose and walked him to the door. "I'm glad you're going to teach Teddy to play baseball. He needs a good role model in his life, even if it's only for a brief time."

He pulled her into his arms and kissed her like he had been aching to do all evening. "I love you, Sprite."

"I love you, too," she told him as he walked out the door. She locked the door and made her way to bed, turning off lights as she went.

CHAPTER FOURTEEN

Brad drove home thinking about Dani and the two children she had taken in. *I hope she doesn't get too attached. He smiled remembering her on the sofa with the two sleeping children. She'd make a wonderful mother. Maybe when this case was over he'd propose. It was time.*

He pulled himself out of his reverie just in time to miss a doe and two fawns. Once at home he made a cup of coffee and pulled out the file Dani had given him. Maybe when he read it, he would have a better understanding of her mission. He might also have a better idea of what he was going to get himself into. He knew as sure as he knew his name he would help her even if he had misgivings.

He got a notepad and a pen. He was going to write down any questions he might have. Once the coffee was ready he sat down and began reading. An hour later he rubbed his eyes, took the cup to the sink, and headed for bed. His mind was spinning with the enormity of the project Dani was getting involved with.

DANI WAS UP earlier than usual. She wanted to check on the children and make sure they were fed and occupied before she started her day. She had much to go over before she called the prosecutor to talk about Theodore Jackman's case. She was hoping to do the best for everyone involved.

She left the kids eating in the kitchen and went to listen to the 9-1-1 call. Dani was shocked to hear Teddy's frantic voice, "Please come quick, I think my dad is going to kill my mom."

> Operator: "Are you someplace safe?"
> Teddy: "Yes, I have my sister and we are in the closet."
> Operator: "Where are your parents?"
> Teddy: "They were in the living room when the yelling started. I can hear my dad hitting her. Please, hurry."
> Operator: "The police are on the way. You just stay on the line with me."
> Teddy: "Send an ambulance, too."
> Operator: "Teddy, they are coming. Listen for the sirens."
> Teddy: "I can hear them but they are far away."
> Operator: "Tell me where you are in the apartment."
> Teddy: "We are in the bedroom closet."
> Operator: "Stay in the closet until the police officer comes to get you. I will stay on the line."
> Teddy: "Okay, just hurry, my mom is crying."
> Operator: "Teddy, they are getting the super to open the door. Stay in the closet."
> There was a pause in the tape. Then Teddy responded: "I hear voices."
> Operator: "Those are the officers, Teddy please, stay where you are."

Teddy: "We are still in the closet. I hear people coming."

Operator: "Teddy, an officer is going to open the closet door now."

Dani heard the door open and a voice say, "Teddy, I'm Officer Stanley. You and your sister can come out now."

Teddy to the operator: "Can I hang up now?"

Operator: "You sure can, Teddy."

The tape ended there. Dani had not realized Teddy had been the caller. She was surprised to find tears running down her cheeks.

"Miss Dani," Teddy ventured, "are you okay?"

Dani had been so engrossed in the tape she had not heard him come in. Looking up now, she became aware of Teddy and Amy standing at her desk. She came out from behind the desk and hugged them both to her. "I'm okay now," she assured him.

"What made you cry?" Amy whispered.

Dani looked at the little girl and said, "I did not know who called 9-1-1. Teddy was really brave."

Amy beamed, "Teddy always takes care of me and calls 9-1-1 when Daddy is being mean."

Teddy blushed at the praise from his sister. Dani looked at him and ruffled his hair.

"Have you had to call very often?" she asked him?

Teddy shrugged, "Maybe four or five times."

"You are good at taking care of Amy and your mom," she acknowledged. "I am very proud of you."

Again, Teddy blushed, "Thank you."

"So, have you decided what you want to do today?" she asked.

Teddy nodded, "Since Mr. Brad is coming on Saturday to play baseball with me can we just play in the backyard today?"

"Yes, you may," Dani told him. "I'll let Ella know where you will be. Please stay close to the house. I will take you to the river later."

"Okay," he said. Taking Amy's hand they headed toward the backdoor and out into the lawn.

Dani snuck a peak out her office window and saw them playing a game of chase. She smiled thinking they would be okay for a while and went back to getting ready to call the prosecutor. Knowing the children had been at risk made her angry.

She went over all the material she had, then called the district attorney's office to make an appointment for later in the day.

Maureen came in and she looked up. Laughter floated in from the backyard, "I take it they are settling in okay?"

"They are sweet kids," Dani replied, "and very resilient. Teddy made the 9-1-1 call to save their mother."

"Are you going to have trouble defending the father?" Maureen asked.

"I don't think so," Dani answered. "He has a prior sentence for a barroom brawl. There are several calls to 9-1-1 concerning spousal abuse. I think I can get him a plea bargain. The hardest thing will be getting him to agree to it."

Maureen smiled, "I'm willing to bet you can make the plea deal look like a picnic."

Dani looked quizzically at Maureen, "I only hope so. Then it will be a matter of getting the family relocated so he cannot find them when he is out."

"You think it will be necessary?" Maureen asked.

"I do," Dani told her. "I have a file for you to look at. When you get to the end you'll find a contract. Please take all the time you need." Handing Maureen the file, Dani left the room.

She headed for the backyard and the children. She thought to have a brief talk with them before leaving for the courthouse. It was important to her they stay in the yard where they could be seen.

Teddy said calmly, "Miss Dani, we will stay right here. Miss Ella told us she would call us for lunch."

Dani ruffled his hair once again, "I knew I could count on you. Amy, listen to Teddy, okay?"

"Yes, Miss Dani," she said in her whisper soft voice.

Dani left them and went back to the office where she picked up her briefcase. "I'll be at the district attorney's office should you need me."

"We'll be fine here," Maureen assured her. "I'm hoping you are successful."

THE DISTRICT ATTORNEY'S office was located in the courthouse. Dani went through the metal detectors then was on her way. The secretary looked up when she entered. "One moment, Miss Montgomery, and I'll tell, Mr. Stamm you are here." She picked up her phone to let the prosecutor know his appointment was here.

Richard Stamm came to his door looking as if he had just stepped off the cover of an exclusive men's magazine. "Miss Montgomery, please come in won't you." He ushered her into his office closing the door behind them.

"Thank you for taking the time to see me," Dani began as she took a seat in front of his desk.

"The pleasure is mine," he gushed. "How can I help you?"

"I'd like to discuss the Jackman case," Dani said pulling a file out of her briefcase. "I'd like to see if we can come up with a plea agreement."

Stamm looked incredulous, "You want a plea deal? You're not taking it to court to try and get him off?"

Dani was unruffled, "I am here to see to a speedy conclusion to this issue. I have seen his previous arrest record, listened to the 9-1-1 recording and spoken to the victim. I believe a plea is in the best interests of my client."

"I had not considered a plea," Stamm told her honestly. "What did you have in mind?"

"After reviewing the case, I see a trial could get him fifteen to thirty years," Dani answered. "I was hoping we could reduce his time to ten to twenty years."

Again Stamm was astonished, "You can't be serious."

"I most assuredly am."

"You could easily ask for less time and hope I'd come up with something in the middle," Stamm told her.

"Mr. Stamm, I am not here to waste time," Dani assured him. "I don't like haggling with someone's life. I came up with what I thought was a reasonable time and one I could sell to my client."

"I agree," Stamm replied. "Your client would be crazy to turn this down. I'll get the papers drawn up."

Dani handed him her papers and gathered her briefcase. Standing, she held out her hand to Richard Stamm, "Thank you for agreeing to meet with me. I'd like the earliest possible trial date and sentencing."

"I'll have a date for you by close of business," Stamm assured her. As she left, he wondered why all cases couldn't go the way this one had. It made him think about what it would be like to go up against Miss Montgomery in court.

DANI WENT FROM the courthouse to the county jail to see Theodore Jackman. Again she went through the metal detector leaving many of her belongings with the guards. Then she was lead to a conference room where she took papers out of her briefcase as she waited for her client.

She did not have long to wait before Theodore Jackman was brought in to see her. She stood and offered her hand to him.

"Is my wife okay?" he asked seating himself across from her.

"She is recovering," Dani assured him.

"So, when can I get out of here?"

"Mr. Jackman, this is your second arrest for assault," Dani began, "I have spoken to the district attorney and he is willing to give you a plea bargain."

"What do you mean a plea bargain?" his angry question startled her.

"I mean if we go to trial with your history, we stand to lose and you will get fifteen to thirty years in prison," Dani told him. "If you take a plea, I can get the sentence reduced to ten to twenty years. As your attorney, I would recommend the plea if you want to see the outside of a prison again."

He hemmed and hawed a few minutes, "You think this is the best deal?"

"Yes, frankly I do."

"Will I be able to see my wife and kids?"

"Not at this time," Dani told him. "Your wife remains in the hospital. She has a broken arm and some cracked ribs."

"Who's got my kids?" he yelled.

The guard poked his head in the door. "We okay in here?"

Dani looked at him, "We're fine. Mr. Jackman was given some bad news."

The guard let himself out.

Looking at him as he tried to control himself she answered, "Your children are being well taken care of, I saw to it myself."

"Okay, then," he said. "What do I have to do?"

"Sign these papers agreeing to the plea arrangement," she told him as she handed him the papers and a pen. "I will know by the end of the day when we will see the judge. I have asked for them to do it speedily."

"Thanks," he grumbled.

She stood and knocked on the door. The guard came in, cuffed Jackman, and led him back to his cell. Dani picked up the papers and pen returning them to her briefcase. She then made her way out of the jail and back to her car. If she hurried, she would make it home in time to have lunch with the children before her afternoon appointment.

Macy had put off reading Dani's proposal. She was not sure she wanted to get involved in Dani's new project. She had set the proposal aside when she got home and did not think about it until today. Maybe it would be okay to at least read it. After her morning routine in the workout room, she made a cup of tea and took the file to the living room.

First came a letter it read:

Macy,

I am starting this project in memory of Michelle. She was a huge part of my decision to become a lawyer. I believed I could win justice for her working as a prosecutor. I see now I was wrong.

My private practice has been more rewarding, but it has not brought me closer to finding justice for Michelle and all the other Michelle's of the world. I have researched this for weeks. I know all there is to know about it. It will be walking a fine line between legal and illegal. I will understand if you don't want to be part of this.

Dani

Macy took a long drink of her tea and thought back to the horrible last year of Michelle's life. It had shaken them to the core of their beliefs. It was the reason she became a police officer. Putting the letter aside, she began reading Dani's proposal. When she came to the end, she found a contract. This was something she was going to talk over with Eli before she signed on. It might be a good course of action for them both.

She reached for her phone to call Eli.

"Patterson," he said answering his phone.

"Good evening to you, too," she said smiling.

"Hi," was his enthusiastic reply.

"I've been reading a proposal Dani gave me and I'd like to hash it over with you. I think it's something we could both get into," she told him.

"Okay," he said with hesitation. "Are you sure this is something I should know about?"

Macy laughed, "Of course, it's not a girl thing. It's a legal thing."

"In that case, when would you like to discuss it?"

"How about as soon as you get here?" she suggested.

"I'm on my way," he said.

Macy heard the dial tone and went to make sure there was wine in the fridge. She also checked to make sure she had cheese and crackers. No longer did her refrigerator seem like the empty elephant it had been. She was even learning to use the crock pot her brother had given her.

Inside of fifteen minutes she heard Eli pull into the driveway. She met him at the front door. He pulled her into his arms for a kiss, then asked, "So, what is this project?"

"Would you like some wine?" Macy asked.

"No, coffee is good," he replied.

She put coffee on and handed him the file she had just finished reading. He sat on the sofa and started reading. Macy brought him coffee and refreshed her tea. She sat curled up next to him saying nothing while he read. Sometimes she could not get over how natural it was to have him with her. She drifted into her own thoughts and was startled when Eli hugged her.

"So, what do you think?" she asked.

"I think she's put a lot of thought into this," he answered cautiously. "You don't often talk about what happened to Michelle. I also know if this brings the two of you some kind of closure, you will most likely do it."

"I asked you to read it, because I'd hoped you would want to be part of it, too," she pouted.

Eli kissed the top of her head, "Who said I wasn't going to be?"

Macy looked him in his beautiful blue eyes, "Do you mean it?"

"Of course," he laughed. "I knew it was important when you called. And I can see how my working with missing kids, might lead to me helping the two of you. Do you know of anyone else she might have brought into this plan?"

"I can't imagine she hasn't conned Brad into helping her," Macy said with conviction. "I don't know if she's told anyone else or not and I don't think I want to know."

"You're right," Eli told her brushing the hair back from her face. "The less we know about those involved the easier it will be."

Macy leaned into him and whispered, "I love you."

He held her close and told her, "I love you, too." After a few minutes he pulled away from her and put all the papers back in the folder. "Do you think you can get me a contract, too?"

"I'm going to sign mine and take it to her tomorrow, I'll pick you up one then," she assured him. "I'm glad you think this is worthwhile."

"Abused women have been at risk for too long," he replied. "If I can do something to save even one, it will be worth it."

He stood pulling her to him for a kiss. Macy knew this kiss would be one to keep her wishing for more. Then let her go saying, "I'll see you for dinner tomorrow."

She walked him to the door and watched him drive away. Then she picked up the papers in the file and found the contract. She signed her name and set it with her purse to take with her tomorrow. This was the best thing she had done since meeting Eli.

Dani made it home just as the children were sitting down to lunch. She had called the prosecutor to tell him, Jackman had agreed to the deal. There would be a hearing tomorrow afternoon. Dani could hardly wait to tell Lizzy Jackman she had ten years to get her life in order and get away from Willow Bend with her children. For now she was going to enjoy some time with those children.

"Miss Dani," Amy exclaimed with glee when she saw Dani enter the room.

"I thought I'd come home for lunch today," Dani said as she took a seat.

Ella came through with a plate and lunch for Dani then left the room. Maureen joined them a few minutes later.

Teddy was thoroughly enjoying all the attention he and his sister were getting. He started chattering about how Mr. Sam was going to teach him gardening this afternoon.

Dani was glad to see Sam had taken a shine to the young boy. He was going to need good male role models in his life. The children kept up a running chatter with Maureen and Dani making the appropriate comments. After lunch Teddy asked to be excused so he could go learn gardening. Amy asked if she could rest in her room. Dani and Maureen headed to the office.

Mr. Bascom showed up for his appointment to go over his will. When he was satisfied, Dani asked Maureen to come witness his signature. Macy had arrived and was also asked to act as a witness.

When Mr. Bascom had gone with his copy of his will, Dani turned to Macy and asked, "What brings you here today?"

Macy produced the contract she'd signed and said, "I'd like one more if it's okay with you."

"Sure," Dani said a puzzled expression on her face.

"It's for Eli," Macy assured her. "He thinks this is a good and worthwhile project and would like to be a part of it."

Dani sat at her computer, pulled up the contract, and printed it. She took Macy's and made a copy for Macy to take with her.

"I'm glad he approves," Dani told her. "I wish I could be so sure Brad does."

Macy rolled her eyes replying, "If Brad didn't approve, you'd be looking for someone less trustworthy to be doing your secret construction."

Both of them laughed. "I'm glad you came, Macy," Dani told her. "I enjoy when we can laugh."

"Me, too, but I'm on lunch so I'm off," Macy told her as she left.

"While you're collecting contracts," Maureen began, "here is mine. I want to be a part of something I think is worthy."

"Thank you, Maureen," Dani said. Again she made a copy for Maureen to keep and put the original with Macy's. "It looks like we'll be in business as soon as the room is finished."

"I think we've already started," Maureen said as she went back to her desk.

Dani took a quick look out the window to see Sam had Teddy loading rocks into a wheelbarrow. She laughed remembering when Sam taught her gardening. *Sam's idea of gardening was to assign her every rock in the lawn to be picked up and put into his wheelbarrow. After a few days, she suspected he put the rocks in different places to keep her busy.*

BRAD SHOWED UP a bit early. If Dani was surprised, she didn't show it. Instead she introduced him to Maureen then led him to her office.

"So, what brings you early?" she asked the curiosity in her voice could not be disguised no matter how nonchalant she attempted to act.

"I thought I'd introduce Teddy to some baseball before dinner," he said smiling. "Then I can sneak off after dinner and get some work done." He winked.

"You are too clever," she acknowledged. "Sam is teaching Teddy to garden, but I'm sure he won't mind a break."

Brad walked up to where she stood at the window wrapping his arms around her he chuckled, "I remember Sam giving me the same lesson the summer we spent together. One rock after another went into the wheelbarrow. I used to think he had rocks brought in just to make more work for me."

She nodded, "Me, too."

"Where is Amy?"

Dani turned in his arms and kissed his cheek, "She decided to take a nap."

"Don't tell me Sam wore her out hauling rocks," he said in mock shock.

"No, she and Teddy were playing chase when I left this morning," Dani assured him.

Brad fumbled in his pocket for a piece of paper, "I also brought the contract you put in the packet. I'm in, Sprite, for the long haul." He handed her his signed contract.

She signed it and made a copy for him. As she handed it to him she put the original in the folder on her desk.

"Are you getting many recruits?" he teased.

"As a matter of fact, it looks like there will be five of us taking on the project," she quipped smiling.

"Good, do I know any of the others?" Brad was serious now.

Dani glanced at him, "Yes, you know them all. You just met Maureen, and we had dinner with Macy and Eli the other night."

"Are there going to be others?" try as he might he could not keep the anxiousness out of his voice.

"I'm not planning on it," she said. "I think this is more than enough people. Maureen and I will be the only ones taking calls on this. We have the biggest stake as we have to work with the network to secure paperwork."

Brad ran his hand through his hair, "I'm trusting you know what you are getting into. Just tell me what you need me to do."

"At the moment, go teach Teddy some baseball," she told him pushing him toward the door. "I still have work to do."

Laughing he headed for the back door and Teddy. She watched until he turned the corner then went to her desk to finish the will for Mrs. Wheeler who would be in tomorrow to sign it.

CHAPTER SEVENTEEN

Teddy was all excited about playing baseball. It was his only topic of conversation at dinner.

"Mr. Brad showed me how to hold the bat," he said the excitement in his voice contagious. "And he showed me how to stand. Then when he threw the ball, I watched it and swung. I hit it! Mr. Brad told me it would be a base hit." He beamed at them full of pride.

"I'm so glad you were able to make a hit," Dani told him. "Now eat your dinner so you can hit more later."

Brad ruffled Teddy's hair, "She's right. You need strong muscles to make the team and lots of practice."

Teddy turned immediately to food. Amy smiled and ate a bit, but Dani noticed her pushing her food around her plate.

"Amy, are you feeling okay?" she asked reaching to feel the child's forehead.

Amy shook her head negatively and put down her fork. "My tummy aches."

"Let's go see if Ella has something to make you feel better." Dani lifted Amy from her seat and headed into the kitchen. She came back a few minutes later saying, "I'm going to put Amy to bed."

Let on their own Brad and Teddy talked baseball. When Dani returned they both looked up expectantly.

"Ella made her some peppermint tea and she is going to lie down for a bit. We put a bucket next to the bed in case she gets sick," Dani told them. "I'll check in on her I a little bit. If this doesn't work, I'll find a doctor to call."

"Amy gets sick sometimes," Teddy told them. "We never take her to the doctor."

"Maybe it's time someone did," Brad suggested.

"Let's see how she feels after a little nap," Dani replied. "What are you two doing this afternoon?"

"I'm going to work with Mr. Sam some more and then practice throwing the baseball," Teddy assured her.

Brad sighed, "Unfortunately, I am going back to work, but I'll be back before bedtime."

They finished their meal and each went off to their afternoon projects.

DANI HAD TROUBLE focusing after dinner. She checked on Amy before leaving for her meeting with the children's mother. Her hope was to prevent Lizzy from worrying, not bring her news of a sick child. Amy was sleeping peacefully and did not feel as though she had a fever.

She asked Maureen, "Do you know a good pediatrician?"

"Sure, Dr. Abby Wellsley," Maureen answered. "Would you like me to call her?"

"Please, I don't think it's an emergency," Dani began, "but I'd like her to give Amy a physical tomorrow."

"I'm on it," Maureen said reaching for the phone.

Dani left to head to the hospital. *How do I explain to Lizzy Amy might be ill? I wonder the last time she had a check-up. Maybe I should ask her.* Arriving at the hospital, Dani put all her anxiety on hold. She stopped in the gift shop and picked up a bed jacket and some flowers in a vase.

Lizzy Jackman was sitting in a chair when Dani entered. Her hair had been washed and she seemed to be doing much better.

"Hi, Lizzy, do you remember me?" Dani asked.

"You're the nice lady who is watching my babies," Lizzy replied.

Dani handed her the bag with the bed jacket in it and set the flowers on the night table. "I hope you are feeling better," she said.

"Much better, thank you," Lizzy replied. "You didn't need to buy me things. How are my babies?'

"Teddy is learning to play baseball and Amy is enjoying some paper dolls," Dani answered. "Lizzy, when did Amy last have a doctor's check-up?"

"Shoot, we don't have money for them," Lizzy said shaking her head.

"I understand, but do you remember the last check-up she had?" Dani pressed.

"Well, I took her to the free clinic for her shots, but she don't need none again until she starts school," she seemed to be thinking as she answered. "Is Amy sick?"

"I don't think so," Dani replied. "She had a little tummy ache at lunch. She was napping when I left."

"Oh, she gets it sometimes," Lizzy affirmed. "I let her sleep and then she's fine."

"See I knew it was nothing," Dani reassured her. "The doctor tells me you will be released next week. I want you to come to my house until you are on your feet again."

"I couldn't," Lizzy began, "you have already been too kind, takin' in my kids. I can't never repay you."

"There is nothing to repay," Dani told her firmly. "I offered to take them in. The offer applies to you until you are on your feet."

"I'll think on it," was Lizzy's noncommittal answer.

"Your husband took a plea deal," Dani stated. "He will be doing at least ten years. Meanwhile we can get you trained to do something and moved to where he cannot find you. I will help you file for divorce. You will be free."

Lizzy's head shot up at this announcement. "How can I ever be free? I gots two little ones to look out for now and no man."

"I'll help you get trained and start a new life, if you'd like," Dani offered.

She shook her head no, "I can't take no more from you. It would be like charity."

"Not if you could earn money while being trained," Dani told her. "Just think about it."

"I'm not makin' no promises," Lizzy stated. "I won't be no charity case."

"Well, I'm not giving up," Dani said just as stubbornly. "I am off to go home."

"Tell my little ones I miss them," Lizzy said the wistfulness in her voice took the edge off Dani's anger.

She took Lizzy's hand, "You'll be with then soon." She walked to the door feeling like she had lost a major battle. Turning for one last glance at Lizzy she saw tears rolling down her cheeks.

Lizzy looked at Dani and mouthed, "Thank you."

<h1 style="text-align:right">CHAPTER EIGHTEEN</h1>

Dani drove home wondering how she was going to get through to Lizzy Jackman and help her become independent. She also was worried something serious might be wrong with Amy. It is not like a child to be frequently ill at dinner time. Well, the doctor could tell her more tomorrow.

She arrived in time to see Brad and Teddy practicing with the baseball and bat. Teddy was getting pretty good at hitting the balls Brad threw. Dani thought Brad was getting extra exercise being the pitcher as well as the outfield. It made her smile.

Inside she found Amy sitting at her desk watching Teddy and Brad out the window. Maureen motioned to Dani as she came in.

"I secured a doctor's appointment tomorrow morning," she told Dani. "Amy has been perched in your seat since she woke up. She won't even eat a cookie or drink milk. I'm worried."

"Does she have a fever?" Dani asked.

"Not so far as I can tell," Maureen told her. "She seems very skittish when I approach your office, so I've just kept an eye on her from here."

"Thanks, Maureen," Dani replied. "Is there any way you might be able to train their mother to work in a law office?"

"Sure," was Maureen's energetic reply. "We'll start with filing and then I'll teach her the different forms and let her practice. After she's got those down we'll work on her answering the phones."

"Great," Dani said. "I have ten years to get her out on her own. I'll pay her a stipend or something while she trains. She won't take charity as she calls it."

Maureen nodded, "I'll make sure she has all the work forms filled out."

Dani found herself smiling as she entered her office to see how Amy was feeling.

"Hello, there, Amy," she said softly as she entered.

"Miss Dani," the child exclaimed as she left her perch and came running. "I thought you left us."

"I went to see your mom," Dani explained picking the little girl up. "She told me to tell you she misses you."

Amy shook her head, "No, she doesn't. She leaves us all the time."

"What do you mean she leaves you all the time?"

"Daddy smacks her and the neighbors take her away," Amy explained. "Teddy has to find us food, because Daddy goes away, too."

"Your daddy won't be smacking anyone for a long time," Dani assured her. "Your mommy is going to come here and stay with us while she gets better."

"She's not getting better," Amy said firmly.

"What makes you say such a thing?" Dani asked.

"She comes home, does bad things, and daddy hurts her again," Amy told her. "She should know better."

Dani shook her head. "Amy, your mommy doesn't do bad things. Your daddy has a sickness and tries to make mommy think she has done something wrong so he has a reason to hit her. There is never a reason to hit another person."

"I know," Amy said softly. "Teddy makes me hide in the closet when Daddy is mad. He doesn't want him to think I'm bad and hit me."

Dani hugged the little girl to her not knowing what to say. Finally she said, "Teddy is a brave boy."

"Yes, he is," Amy agreed.

Dani put her down and said, "Let's go see about a snack."

LATER, DANI SUPERVISED baths for the children, then read to them before tucking them in for the night. With lights out she headed back downstairs. Brad had made a big show of leaving, then gone in through the cave door to work in the chamber. Dani knew he would work later than usual to make up for lost time. The children had grown on him as much as they had her.

Dani's plan was to teach Lizzy how to run a small law office. She would help Lizzy get a divorce and learn a skill so she could find a job in a new town. She would suggest Lizzy change their last name legally so her ex would not be able to find her when he was released. Teddy and Amy were young enough to find a place for themselves in a new home. She had ten years to make it and maybe find someone to be a good father to her children. Dani was just going to put her in a position to make a better life for herself. The good thing was Maureen was on board for helping her.

Brad wandered in an hour later. Dani looked up and asked, "Would you like a drink?"

"Not tonight, Sprite," he replied.

She came over to where he was standing, his hair was still damp from his shower. Again she took in the fresh manly scent of him and felt her heartbeat pick up.

He took her in his arms just holding her. "Dani, I love you," he whispered. "I don't want to see you get hurt."

Dani tilted her head to look at him, "They are Lizzy's children and are only here until she can get on her feet. Maureen is going to teach her how to run a small law office. "I'll pay her a part-time wage until she feels ready to branch out. To begin with, she has a broken leg, a broken arm, and cracked ribs. She won't be able to do much."

He kissed her lightly. "My ears hear what you are saying," he told her. "But I know you are one who loves deeply and you love these two kids."

"Someday I will have my own children to love," Dani countered. "For now I'm going to do all I can to help these two and their mother find a better life."

They walked to the front door. Dani followed Brad out onto the porch. He took her in his arms for a deep kiss. Lifting her off the ground and holding her as if he could melt her into his skin. Then he gently set her down. "Goodnight, Sprite." He left her standing there and walked to his truck.

CHAPTER NINETEEN

Morning was busy as Dani was taking Amy to see Dr. Wellsley. Hopefully it was nothing, but she wanted to be sure. Breakfast was hurried, seeing Teddy off to work with Sam was next. Making sure she had no pressing appointments and getting Amy into the car completed the hectic morning.

Arriving at the doctors Dani was bombarded with a ton of paperwork to fill out. Most of it she had no idea. She asked Amy a few questions, but it seemed the child didn't have the answers either. Going to the doctor seemed foreign to her. While she was a bit apprehensive, she seemed to enjoy the toys there for her to play with.

"I feel unequipped for this," Dani told the receptionist when she took the papers back up. "I don't know her medical history. Only her mother did tell me her shots were up-to-date according to the health department."

The receptionist nodded and said, "If you'll sign this form, we can request records from the health department."

Dani quickly signed the form, then returned to her seat. She watched Amy play as others were called in for their appointments. Time passed pleasantly, Amy put away the toys and curled up on Dani's lap.

"Is it my turn yet?" she asked.

"Soon, baby, soon," Dani assured her.

Moments later the door opened, a mother and child walked out and the nurse called, "Amy Jackman."

Dani carried Amy into the hallway.

"I'm Dr. Wellsley's nurse, Sue," she said. "Will you follow me please?"

Dani followed with Amy clinging to her. They entered a small room and Sue said, "Amy can you stand on the scales for me?"

It took a minute, but Dani set her down and she climbed on to the scales.

"How old are you?" Sue asked.

"Four," Amy answered.

"You seem to be a little small for a four year old," she commented making notes on the chart. "Let's see how tall you are." She brought down a measuring tool to see how tall Amy was. "Hmmm, forty inches," Sue said again making notes. "Okay, Amy, can you hop up on this table?"

Amy first looked to Dani who nodded yes, then climbed up on the table. "Now I'm going to take your blood pressure," Sue told her. "When I'm done, I'll let you listen to your heart."

She placed a small blue cuff around Amy's arm and inflated it. She took the blood pressure and as promised showed Amy how to listen to her heart. After that she took Amy's temperature, looked in her ears, and throat.

"We are now going to an exam room where the doctor will come in to see you," Sue told her.

Amy climbed down and went to Dani taking her hand as they followed Sue to yet another room. "You wait here and Dr. Wellsley will be right in." Then she left them.

"I wish there were toys here," Amy said flatly.

Dani smiled saying, "I'm sure it won't be long now."

It was not long and there came a knock on the door. "Come in," Amy said softly.

A young woman with coal black hair peeked around the door, "Hello, I'm Dr. Wellsley." She looked between Dani and Amy then looked at Amy saying, "You must be Amy."

Nodding her head yes, she moved slightly closer to Dani. Dr. Wellsley noted this and said, "I need to examine you to see if we can find out why you keep getting tummy aches. Will it be okay?"

Again Amy just nodded.

"Will you climb up on this little bed?" the doctor asked.

She looked first at Dani who nodded, then climbed up on the bed. "Is it going to hurt when you zamine me?" she whispered.

"I don't think so," the doctor assured her. Then she looked at Dani saying, "If you'd like to stand next to her and hold her hand, it's okay."

Relieved, Dani rose to stand next to Amy. Amy took her hand smiling tentatively.

"Can you tell me when your tummy hurts the most, Amy?" asked the doctor.

"When I eat," Amy replied.

"Every time you eat?" the doctor pressed.

"Yes, but sometimes it hurts more," Amy told her.

Dani felt tears sting her eyes, guilt plagued her, because she had not seen something was wrong with Amy.

As Amy lay on the exam table the doctor felt her tummy with her hands. At one point, Amy made a hissing sound. "Is this where it hurts?" the doctor asked.

"Yes," she whispered.

Dr. Wellsley whispered back, "I have some good news. I have some medicine for you to fix this all up."

Amy smiled from ear-to-ear. "Miss Dani, they can fix me," the wonder in her voice was not lost on either of the women.

Turning to Dani, Dr. Wellsley said, "We need to make this child's life less stressful, she has the beginning of an ulcer. I have medication she needs to take before every meal. I will give you several refills. It should coat her stomach and allow her to eat, something I think she will enjoy." She smiled at Amy.

"Oh, yes," Amy agreed.

Dani let go of the breath she was holding. She could handle this. "Thank you, Dr. Wellsley,"

"You are welcome," the doctor replied. "Now Amy, if you don't feel well, please tell someone so, I can check up on you."

"I will." Amy sat up and hugged Dani. "I like her."

"So do I, Pumpkin," Dani assured her hugging her back.

The doctor wrote out a prescription then Dani and Amy were on their way.

BACK AT HOME, Amy skipped happily to the back yard. Dani headed to her office to see what had happened while she was out. She was surprised to see a woman waiting for her.

"Miss Dani, this is Margo Hunter," Maureen told her.

"Ms. Hunter, please come into my office," Dani said inviting her to follow her in. She closed the door saying, "Please take a seat. I apologize for keeping you waiting."

"It's okay," Ms. Hunter said flatly. "I understood your little girl was sick."

"Not my daughter," Dani corrected. "Just a child under my care. Now, how can I help you?"

Ms. Hunter hesitated then removed the scarf and dark glasses she was wearing. Dani let out a gasp when she saw the bruises the woman had been hiding.

"I didn't mean to startle you," she said.

"It's okay," Dani reassured her. "I wasn't expecting you to be injured."

"A police report was filed," Ms. Hunter continued. "My husband was arrested and is in jail until he can get a lawyer."

"May I ask what brought you to me?" Dani wanted to know.

"A lady in the emergency room the night I was taken in," she replied. "I went to check on her and she told me you were taking care of her bills so she could heal."

"Lizzy Jackman," Dani said. "It's her daughter who was ill."

Ms. Hunter nodded, "I need to get away before he comes back. I don't know if you can help me or not, but can you point me to someone who can?"

"Do you have any skills so you can support yourself? Do you have children?" Dani asked. "And when is your husband's arraignment?"

"I am a hair dresser, or I was before I got married," she said. "I don't have children. My husband is being arraigned in the morning."

"I'll see if I can get his case assigned to me," Dani told her. "Once I know more about him and the situation, I can see how to best help you."

"Can you help me and represent my husband?" Ms. Hunter asked.

"I can represent your husband in his abuse case," Dani responded. "You came to me about getting away, it's a different issue."

"Will you be able to get me a divorce?" she wanted to know.

"If you want one, yes," Dani answered.

"Thank you," Ms. Hunter replied. "I won't take any more of your time."

"I'll have Maureen schedule you an appointment in a couple days and we should have the papers for your divorce and a plan for helping you get fresh start," Dani told her standing and holding out her hand.

Ms. Hunter took her hand. After a firm shake the two women went to the outer office. "Maureen, Ms. Hunter will need an appointment in a couple of days and will you book me into court tomorrow morning, please?"

"I'll get right on it," Maureen said reaching for the appointment book.

CHAPTER TWENTY

Brad came early again to toss the baseball to Teddy. Amy was playing quietly in her room. Dani had taken care of the latest will and it was filed away.

Ella came into the office.

"May I speak to Miss Dani?" she asked.

Maureen looked startled saying, "Ella, you don't need permission to speak to Miss Dani. Her door is open and she would welcome a break I'm sure."

"Thank you," she said and walked into Dani's office. She closed the door softly. "Miss Dani?"

Dani looked up, "Ella, is something wrong?"

Ella took a seat in one of the chairs in front of Dani's desk. Wringing her hands she began, "My niece, is in trouble and she needs help."

"What kind of trouble?" Dani asked already reaching for a legal pad and pen.

"The man she lives with, hit her," Ella said. "She needs to get away where he won't find her."

"What kind of work skills does she have?" Dani began.

"She went to college to study art," Ella replied. "I can't see where she makes any money at it."

"Can she teach art?" was Dan's next question.

"Not like in school," Ella said. "She has no teaching degree."

"She doesn't need one to give art lessons," Dani assured her.

"I suppose she could then," Ella's answer was hesitant.

"Where does she live?" Dani asked.

"She lives in Rivers Edge," Ella confirmed.

"Can you get her to come talk to me?" Dani was anxious to see this woman quickly.

"I can ask her to come," Ella said.

Dani nodded, "Let's get her here tomorrow afternoon if we can. The sooner I get to work on this the safer she will be. I could call my friend Macy and have her look in on her if you'd like."

Ella nodded, "I wish someone would check on her. Misty can be real stubborn at times."

"You give me her address and I'll see if Macy can stop by and check on her or get someone to stop by," said Dani. "Then invite her here tomorrow afternoon and I'll see what I can do."

"Thank you, Miss Dani," the relief in Ella's voice was evident to Dani.

The two women walked to the door. Ella hugged Dani saying, "I'm so proud of you."

Dani smiled as she opened the door. "Maureen, Ella's going to give you some information on her niece. I'm expecting her tomorrow afternoon."

"Sure thing," Maureen chirped. She pulled her appointment book and a sheet of paper for the information she would need from Ella.

BRAD AND TEDDY made their way in to wash up for dinner. Amy was given her little cup of medicine to take. They all made their way to the dining room. Ella brought in the main dish and left Dani to serve. She left for salad and vegetable.

"Miss Dani, dessert is in the kitchen," Ella said.

"Thank you, Ella," Dani said handing a plate to Amy. "You and Sam enjoy your evening."

Ella left and eating began. Tonight's conversation was more subdued as everyone concentrated on their food. Even Amy showed a good appetite. After they were done, Dani took plates to the kitchen and came back with dessert. Ella had made butterscotch pudding. Dani saw chocolate chips on the top and knew the children would be pleasantly surprised by chocolate chips in the pudding, too.

After dinner Dani and the kids pulled out some board games. Brad headed for the chamber to work. He would be able to start painting tomorrow and then he could put in flooring. The room was really shaping up. Dani would need to buy furnishings and stock it with food, but he was beginning to think she could pull this off. He had found a small furnace and put it in. It was electric and drew off the water already coming into the chamber. He had found a way to run the water pipes under the floor to keep the floors warm, too. He had hoped Dani would be able to help him paint. Now the kids were in her care he didn't know if it would be possible.

After putting the kids to bed, Dani wandered to her office to see what information she had on Ella's niece. She also called and left voice mail for Macy. Her message was brief but she asked if Macy could keep an eye on Misty Evons and left the address.

She fixed herself a drink as she waited for Brad. She missed being able to sneak down and watch him work. While sitting there she began day dreaming about what it would be like to marry Brad and have children with him. He was good with Teddy and Amy, so she was pretty sure he would be good with his own children. Funny she had never asked if he wanted children. Maybe she should. Maybe he would not and it would break her heart.

Brad walked in to see tears running down her cheeks as she stared off into space. He wished he could read her thoughts.

"Dani," he whispered coming closer to her.

She wiped her eyes and brought herself out of her reverie. "I'm sorry," she said, "Would you like a drink?"

"I'll get it," he told her walking to the bar. "Are you okay?"

"Just lost in my thoughts," she replied.

"Not happy thoughts, then?" he asked.

"Disconcerting but not unhappy thoughts," was her reassurance.

"Are you getting to close to the children?" he asked turning to face her and taking a drink.

She laughed, "No, I understand they are not mine."

Brad felt her answer was honest, "Good to know you understand. I am ready to start painting the chamber."

"Darn, I wanted to be able to help you," the disappointment in her voice matched the frown on her face.

"What if we start painting at 6:30 tomorrow morning and I join all of you for breakfast at 8?" Brad suggested.

"I'll bring the coffee and meet you in the chamber," she said.

Brad nodded taking another swallow of his drink, "I'm going to come up the river so no one hears me."

Dani nodded, put down her drink, and came toward him. "I'll be ready."

He put his drink on the counter and took her in his arms. "I love you more than you know."

"I think I have an idea," she smiled up at him. Then she stopped smiling. "I want to ask you something."

Brad noted the seriousness in her voice, "Ask."

"Do you ever think about having children?"

He laughed, "Only if you will have them with me." He hugged her to him not waiting for an answer.

When he stopped chuckling he smiled and kissed her. Dani knew he had just sealed his promise with his kiss. Her heart swelled with love. She walked him to the door and as he drove away, she wished with all her heart his days of leaving her would someday be over.

CHAPTER TWENTY-ONE

When her alarm went off at five a. m. Dani wanted nothing more than to hit the snooze button. Instead, she leaped out of bed, dressed in her grubbiest clothes, checked on the children, and headed to the kitchen to make coffee. Once she had a pot done she transferred it to a huge thermos, packed up two cups, sugar and cream, and made her way back up to the closet. She slipped inside and let herself into the hidden tunnel. It was nice to have lights now and not have to juggle a flashlight.

She surveyed all Brad had done, sitting her supplies on a make-shift table. She poured two cups of coffee adding cream and sugar to both and headed for the cave entrance. She unlocked the door and stepped out into the early morning sun.

Walking to the dock she sat down putting both cups beside her and listened for the sound of Brad's boat coming up river. She had less than ten minutes to wait before she heard the sound of his motor across the water. It was another ten minutes before she could see him in the distance.

She moved the coffee cups out of the way and stood ready to tie off his boat when he docked. Once they had the boat tied off, she handed him a cup of coffee.

"Thanks," he said producing a small bag. "I knew you'd need more than coffee."

Dani snatched the bag chuckling, "What have we here?"

"Jelly donuts," Brad told her. "Just save me one."

"One?" she quipped. "Did you sneak into them already?"

Brad blushed, "Naturally."

She looped her arm through his and they headed for the cave entrance. Once inside Dani asked, "How soon can we be ready for cargo?"

The question caught Brad off guard, "Well, as soon as the paint is up and we have furniture, I guess."

"Let's get this done then," Dani said heading for a paint can and paint brush.

"I did the ceiling all the way through last night," Brad told her. "I knew you'd want to start on the walls."

"What color are the walls?" she asked.

"Well," Brad said anticipating her reaction. "I thought this one for the bathroom." He opened a can revealing a tropical shade of blue.

She clapped her hands, "I love it."

"Let's knock this room out," Brad said. "It shouldn't take me more than half an hour. I'll start cutting in then you can roll."

Dani stepped back so Brad could start as soon as he finished cutting in one wall she began to roll paint on it and he began cutting in the next wall. Above the lights and door frame Brad used a small roller. He would install the medicine cabinet as soon as they put the second coat of paint on the walls.

Dani stepped out of the bathroom and wiped her forehead. "I'm glad it's done."

"We'll let it dry and start cutting in the main room," Brad told her.

"And the color is…" He made a huge production of revealing the color to her. It was the softest yellow she had ever seen.

Eyes sparkling she asked, "Can we get this room done this morning?"

"I hope at least one coat and then the second coat in the bathroom," Brad replied. He began cutting in the walls. Dani readied herself to roll paint on as soon as he finished one wall. Together they worked quickly and efficiently. As soon as he had the room cut in he began the second coat in the bathroom. When he finished he returned to the main chamber and helped Dani finish the first coat of paint there.

They cleaned up and headed up the stairs to find the kids and have breakfast.

BREAKFAST WENT BY quickly. Brad pulled up his courage and asked, Dani, "What do you think of Teddy going to work with me today?"

"Fabulous, if Teddy wants to go," she replied smiling.

"Can I work with you?" Amy asked looking at Dani.

"Not today, honey, I have to go to court," Dani replied. "But, I'll bet Miss Maureen could teach you what she does to help me."

Amy beamed at the thought of doing something to help Dani. "I'll do a good job."

"Of course, you will," Dani said giving the shy little girl confidence.

Once they had the day settled, everyone scrambled to get ready. Teddy got dressed. He and Brad set off around the house to take the boat back to town. Amy decided she needed a dress today, then presented herself to Miss Maureen for her duties. Dani quickly changed into a suit then headed for her office to brief Maureen and grab her briefcase. She would step up when Mr. Hunter was arraigned.

Maureen was happy to assist in Amy's training as a legal assistant. Even if she chose a different line of work when she grew up at least she would have skills to fall back on.

With everyone settled in for the day, Dani headed out the front door and on to the courthouse.

DANI WENT THROUGH the courthouse screening process on auto pilot. She took a seat in the courtroom near the front. She wanted to be ready when Mr. Hunter came up for arraignment.

The bailiff asked them all to rise as the judge entered. Dani rose with everyone else. The judge told them to be seated and had the first case called. Dani was in luck Mr. Hunter was brought to the defense table as the bailiff called the case.

"Mr. Hunter do you have counsel?" the judge asked.

Dani rose saying, "Your honor, I have been retained as counsel for Mr. Hunter."

"Approach Ms. Montgomery," the judge ordered.

Dani stepped up to the defense table and whispered, "Your wife hired me."

"Damn bitch," Mr. Hunter yelled. "Does she think I'm made of money?"

"Whispering Dani told him, "I'm working pro bono, Mr. Hunter, there is no cost to either of you. Please be quiet."

Hunter stood there.

"Are we ready, Ms. Montgomery," the judge asked.

"We are Your Honor," she replied.

"People on bail," the judge asked.

"The people are seeking remand," Richard Stamm said. "Mr. Hunter is a repeat offender. This time beating his wife to unconsciousness."

"Ms. Montgomery?" the judge asked.

"We concur for the moment," she replied.

Hunter hissed at her side. She ignored him.

"Mr. Hunter, you will remain in custody until this comes to trial," the judge said bringing down his gavel.

As Mr. Hunter was led away, Dani turned to Richard Stamm. "How soon can I get the file on this?"

"Are you going for a plea deal again?" he asked.

"It depends on what I see in the file and how my client feels about one," Dani replied.

"I'll have the file messengered to you before lunch," Stamm told her. "I expect some kind of answer in twenty-four hours.

"Fair enough," she told him. She turned and left the courtroom. She headed for the police department where she would obtain all the prior records on Mr. Hunter. Once she had them, she headed for home.

Dani made her way back to her office. She found Maureen and Amy taking a morning cookie break.

"How's the helper been?" she asked.

Maureen set her coffee cup down answering, "Best helper I've ever had."

Amy beamed, her little milk mustache widening with her smile.

"I'm glad to hear it," Dani replied. "Anything I should know about?"

"Detective McVannel sent you a fax, we put it on your desk," Maureen told her as Dani walked into her office.

"Thank you," she said walking to the desk to pick up the file.

She put down her brief case as she sat at her desk. Picking up the file she opened it to begin reading about Misty's husband. It was then she noticed Amy at the side. Setting down the file she looked at the little girl.

"We saved you some cookies," Amy said handing her a plate.

"Thank you, very much," Dani answered taking the plate. She selected a cookie and set the plate down. Maureen appeared with a steaming cup of coffee and set it on the desk.

"Amy, are you ready to help me file some papers?" Maureen asked.

"Yes, Miss Maureen, I just wanted Miss Dani to have some cookies," she replied rounding the desk to follow Maureen to the next task.

Dani smiled watching them go. She picked up a cookie, took a bite and reached for the file she had put down. After reading a few minutes she took some notes. Then she picked up the phone to make a call. After the call, Dani went in search of Ella.

She had not wanted to bring Ella into her inner circle of people knowing about the underground chamber, but now she didn't feel she had a choice. She found Ella in the kitchen doing dishes.

"Miss Dani, do you need something?" Ella asked.

"Yes, Ella," she replied. "You and I need to take a walk. I have something I need to talk to you about."

Ella dried her hands and took off her apron. "I'm ready."

The two women went out the back door into the yard. "I want to walk down to the river," Dani began. "I have to show you something and then we need to talk about Misty."

"Yes, Miss Dani," Ella said worry in her voice.

They walked in silence for a while then Dani started, "As a young girl, I often went missing."

Ella laughed, "I do remember."

"I was never out of earshot," Dani confessed. "I just found a hidden place to play."

Ella was puzzled for a minute but followed Dani into a brushy area. There Dani took a key and unlocked a door Ella had never seen before.

"What is this place, Miss Dani?" Ella asked.

"It used to be an old tunnel used for smuggling slaves to the north," Dani told her. "It was also a wonderful hiding place for a young girl who needed time to herself."

"This door looks new," Ella stated.

"It is and I'm going to swear you to secrecy," Dani told her flipping a light switch.

They walked slowly down the hall to the main chamber. Ella looked around in awe. She checked out the bathroom and the main chamber. It was obvious to her someone had been working down here.

"What are you going to smuggle, Miss Dani?" was Ella's suspicious question.

"People," Dani answered. "I am going to rescue women and children from abusive relationships and give them a start on a new life."

"Is this why Mr. Brad has been here in the evenings?" Ella demanded.

"Yes," Dani answered. "He has done all the hard work. We painted this morning."

"You were the ghost the maids all heard," Ella said as things clicked together for her. "How are you going to keep the maids from knowing now?"

"Brad took care of it," Dani assured her. "He put in extra insulation for warmth and sound proofing so those who come here can talk normally."

"So, why are you telling me about this now?" Ella asked.

"I think your niece is going to be one of my first visitors," Dani told her. "I don't think her husband will go for a plea deal, which means he could be out sooner rather than later."

Ella gasped. "Does she know this?"

"Not yet," Dani told her. "I need to get beds, refrigerator, TV, and food in here before I can have guests. We still need to put in the flooring. Brad is hoping to do much of it tonight."

"Miss Dani, you going to kill that man before he can ask you to marry him," Ella scolded.

Dani laughed. "I'm not worried. I help when I can, but I don't want the children to know about this."

"No, I suspect you don't," Ella agreed. "How can I help?"

"I need you to find me some food to store here," Dani began. "I will also need bedding and some cooking pots and utensils."

"I'll get on it right away," Ella told her. "How soon do we need it?"

"As soon as you can get things together," Dani replied. "Keep in mind, there may be kids at times."

"I can take care of it," she answered with assurance.

"Okay, I guess we can head into the house then," Dani said leading the way to the house entrance.

Ella was amazed to learn the tunnel came out in the linen closet. She said, "I'll get to rearranging this closet and put linens for the room closest to the door."

"Thank you, Ella," Dani said giving the woman a hug.

They headed down the stairs, Ella to make a list of the things she would need and Dani to her office to see what else she needed to do.

MAUREEN AND AMY greeted Dani with a package, she took it knowing it would be from the district attorney with information on Mr. Hunter. She took it and headed for her office, she wanted to prepare the best case and worst case scenario for the man so he would see reason and take a plea.

"Miss Dani," Amy hesitated in the doorway, "would it be okay if I took a nap after lunch?"

Dani looked up, "Of course, Pumpkin."

"Good because I'm tired of being a 'ssistant today," the little girl told her.

"You've been a great assistant," Dani assured her. "If you want to go see Miss Ella and ask about lunch you may."

"Thank you," Amy beamed as she skipped away.

Maureen came to stand in the doorway, "Have I lost my assistant?"

"It appears she would like a nap," Dani told her.

"She's been a trooper," Maureen said smiling.

"I'm glad," Dani answered. "I was afraid I was taking advantage of you."

"Never," Maureen affirmed. "She reminded me of all the things I need to remember to teach her mom."

Dani glanced at Maureen, "You'll remember everything when the time comes."

Maureen nodded and went back to her desk.

Dani returned to the packet Stamm had sent. Evan Hunter had quite a long list of prior arrests. Most of them had been for beating on his wife. It made Dani wonder how a person had this much anger.

When she was done with her presentation, she called the district attorney and made an appointment for early tomorrow morning. She'd see Evan Hunter after her meeting with the DA and then would see about what kind of plea bargain she could get him to take.

Maureen came to the door, "Miss Dani, I'm off for the day. Is there anything you need for morning?"

"No, Maureen, thank you," Dani said.

Maureen left and Dani went to check on Amy. The little girl was just waking up.

"Miss Dani, did you need me for something," she asked.

"No, Princess," Dani assured her. "I was just checking on you."

"Oh," Amy said sitting up and swinging her feet over the side of the bed.

"You sound disappointed," Dani said.

Amy shook her head, "I just want to be helpful."

Dani took the child in her arms, "Amy, you just need to be a little girl." She set Amy down and the two of them headed downstairs.

Brad and Teddy were just arriving as the women came down the stairs.

"Isn't that the most beautiful sight you've ever seen, Teddy?" Brad asked looking up the stairs.

"It's just Amy and Miss Dani," Teddy replied.

Brad chuckled, "You are absolutely right, Teddy. For a minute I thought I'd seen two angels."

Teddy rolled his eyes at Brad as if to say, 'Yeah whatever.' But he watched his sister and Dani come down the stairs to join them.

The four of them went into the dining room.

CHAPTER TWENTY-THREE

Brad helped Dani get the kids ready for bed. Teddy had almost fallen asleep at dinner. Amy wanted to hear a story and Brad sat on the edge of her bed, picked up the first book he saw, and began reading *Of Moonbeams and Fairies, Collected Tales by Rebecka Vigus*. He wasn't completely through the first story when Dani took the book from him.

"Wha…." he started.

"Shh," she said putting her finger to her lips. Then she nodded in the direction of the sleeping children.

Brad smiled as she led him from the room.

"They are set for the night," Dani told him. "Shall we finish painting?"

"Sounds like a good plan," he agreed opening the linen closet door.

They made their way to the chamber, set up the paint and began. Since the bathroom had been finished the night before Brad began putting down floor tiles. He would hook up the toilet, sink, and put in the vanity before leaving. It took the better part of two hours before they finished. Dani surveyed the room.

"As soon as we get the floor in here, it'll be ready for furnishings," she stated.

"I'll do it first thing in the morning before the kids get up," Brad assured her. "I can have breakfast with you and head off to work."

"Brad," Dani stepped closer to him. "You're not leaving tonight."

He hesitated before pulling her into his arms, "Are you sure? The kids are here now."

Laughing Dani leaned back in the circle of his arms, "Oh, I'm sure. Sure you're staying the guest room at the end of the hall."

Pulling her to him he chuckled as he whispered, "Minx," in her ear.

Dani smiled and kissed him. As he kissed her back, she felt her heart start slamming in her chest. It was matched by the beat of his own heart. When the kiss ended they clung to each other.

"Okay so maybe this wasn't a good idea," Dani said when she regained her breath.

"It was a good idea," Brad retorted. "Just not good timing."

She looked at him, "Will it ever be?"

"Yes." He pulled her to him again, "Yes, I promise. But let's head upstairs for now."

Together they followed the hall leading to the linen closet. Dani pulled towels off the shelf and handed them to Brad. He went to the bathroom for his shower and she went to check on the kids. Both were sound asleep and she silently left the room. She heard the shower running in the guest bathroom and grabbed towels so she could shower in the main bath.

Brad was waiting in the hallway when she came out. "I just wanted to say goodnight," he said sheepishly.

Dani walked to him, stood on tiptoe, and kissed him soundly. Then stepping back she said, "Goodnight, Brad." Turning before she could change her mind and ravish him in the hallway.

Brad watched her walk to her room knowing it would not take much to make this the right time. He also knew it was not what he wanted for them. When she closed the door he padded down the hall to his room for the night. He knew sleep would not come easily.

MORNING CAME EARLY, Dani was tempted to hit the snooze button when she remembered Brad was just down the hall. She sprang from her bed, hastily tossed on old jeans and a t-shirt, then headed for the kitchen. She stopped short when she smelled the aroma of fresh brewed coffee. Hesitantly she opened the kitchen door. Ella turned at the sound.

"Do you need two cups of coffee this morning?" she asked.

Dani heard the disapproval in her voice. Before she could answer Brad said, "Good morning, ladies." He pecked Dani on the cheek and walked to Ella. He leaned down to kiss her cheek and whispered, "I did not dishonor her." He made his way to the cupboard and took down two cups.

Silently Ella filled both cups. She got cream from the refrigerator and sugar from another cupboard bringing it to them she muttered, "And with small children in the house."

Knowing it would do no good to protest, Dani turned to Brad, "Shall we paint?"

He nodded picking up his cup and following her out of the kitchen. The last words he heard Ella mutter were, "Fools, kidding themselves."

Once in the basement they went to work putting in the flooring. Dani handing Brad the pieces he needed to put down. Working together it took them the better part of an hour and a half to finish.

Standing up Dani said, "I like it. Tomorrow Amy and I are going to shop for furniture, bedding, and other staples."

Brad looked at her and smiled, "I think you need end tables, a table and chairs for eating, towels, a small fridge, linens, and eating utensils."

"What about beds?" Dani asked.

"I've been working on those," he said confidently. "I just need to bring them tomorrow and install them."

"You built the beds?" Dani's expression was priceless.

Brad nodded. "I took the dimensions and built a loft. It will rise above the rest of the room and you'll be able to sleep two there. Then I picked up a daybed to double as a sofa during the day. It will sleep two as it is a trundle. One mattress is beneath and can be pulled out as needed. I also snared a cooktop, I'll install."

"Wow," for once Dani was speechless.

"I think I like this," he told her.

Dani flung herself into his arms almost knocking him down. "I think I love you."

"You only think you do?" he questioned smiling at her.

She shook her head, "I know I do. I just never expected you to do all this."

"In for a penny, in for a pound," was the only cliché he could find to fit the moment.

Together they picked up and headed out the tunnel to the river. Once outside with the door locked. Dani took Brad's hand. "I cannot tell you how happy I am to have your support for this project."

"You knew all along I'd give in and help," Brad remarked.

"I knew you would help," she agreed. "What I didn't know is how much you would help. I appreciate it more than you know."

Together they walked around the house and entered. As they did the children came barreling down the stairs.

"Mr. Brad, did you come to have breakfast?" Amy asked.

"I did if you don't mind," he answered picking her up.

"Nope, it's okay if Miss Dani says you can come," she told him.

Dani smiled saying, "I do believe it would be a good idea."

Teddy was just rolling his eyes.

"What's wrong, Teddy?" Dani asked.

"Love stuff," he answered. "It's like on TV."

They went into the dining room where Ella had placed waffles with all the trimmings and settled in to eat.

After they finished, Teddy went out to help Sam, Brad left for work, Amy made her way to her room where she took out her paper dolls, and Dani went to get herself ready for court.

They were settling into a routine, Dani mused as she drove into town. *She wished she had more time to spend with the children. Yet she knew staying with her gave them stability.*

She pulled into the jail parking lot, went through the procedure of signing in. While she waited for Ethan Hunter to be brought to her, she took the papers she needed him to sign out of her brief case.

The door opened and Ethan Hunter was led in. They chained one of his hands to the desk as he sat across from her. Once done the guards left the room.

"So," Ethan began, "how did my wife con you into working for free?"

"She didn't con me," Dani replied. "I have spoken to the district attorney. Given your past scuffles with the law, he is asking for twenty-five to life."

Ethan scoffed, "And he thinks I won't get off? My wife won't testify against me. They'll drop the charges like they always do."

Dani looked him in the eye before answering, "Not this time, Mr. Hunter. Your wife has already given her deposition to the district attorney. They pulled the number of times police were sent to your house. She is tired of being your punching bag."

"Stupid slut," Ethan raged. "I'll beat her senseless next time."

"You should not be telling me this," Dani assured him. "I have drawn up a plea bargain I believe would be in your best interest. It would give you ten to fifteen years with time off for good behavior. You could be out in five to seven years."

Ethan tried to rise, "You must be out of your mind! I'm not doing time for this shit. Keeping my wife in line is my job as a husband."

Dani began putting papers back in her briefcase, "I will see you in court. I had hoped to make this easy for you, but your attitude will sink you with a jury. Many don't like the idea of a man hitting a woman." She started to rise.

"Wait," he said. "This is the best you can get me?"

"It is."

"What do I have to do?" he asked.

"Sign the papers I have here," Dani said taking papers back out. "On Monday morning you will be required to admit in open court you beat your wife. Then the judge will rule on the plea agreement."

"It's as easy as that?" he asked.

"Yes, it is." Dani put the papers in front of him and slid the pen to him.

Reluctantly Ethan signed the papers. She put them and the pen back in her briefcase and rose to knock on the door. The guards entered. Ethan was cuffed and chained, while the other guard led Dani out.

Once outside she stood letting the wind blow across her face. She really hated being in the jail. She could understand how men and women went crazy being locked up. Today, however she had gained at least five years for Margo Hunter to get her life together and get away from here. She headed to the district attorney's office to let Richard Stamm know what to expect. Both Theodore Jackman and Ethan Hunter would be sentenced on Monday.

CHAPTER
TWENTY-FOUR

Dani returned home to find Brad, Teddy, and Amy in the yard playing baseball. Teddy let out a whoop when he saw her.

"Miss Dani," he yelled, "did you know girls could play baseball, too?"

She laughed, "Yes, Teddy, I knew."

"Well, Amy's not too good yet," he replied.

"Give her time," Brad admonished. "You've had a week to practice."

Amy stood off to the side with a bat in her hand. She was waiting for Mr. Brad to toss the ball to her.

"Okay, Amy," Brad said turning to the little girl, "Let's show Miss Dani what you can do."

Gently he tossed the ball and Amy swung the bat. Dani was pleased to see she connected with it. While the ball barely made it back to Brad, at least Amy had hit it.

"Good job, Amy," Dani cheered.

Amy beamed. Her smile lighting her whole face.

"I'm going to put my briefcase in my office, check to see if I have anything to do, and then change," Dani told them heading to the house.

"Miss Dani," Teddy called, "Mr. Brad asked us to go to dinner and the movies with him. Will you come with us?"

Looking over Teddy's head she saw the plea on Brad's face. "Of course, Teddy. I'd love to go," she answered smiling.

She turned heading to the house, leaving the three of them to practice more baseball while she finished her day.

MAUREEN CAUGHT HER up on the day's news. She would need to return a call to Macy, but otherwise the office was closed for the day.

"Go home, Maureen," Dani told her. "It's been a good start to our becoming known in town."

"Are you still going to work?" Maureen asked.

"I am going to put the two files for Monday in my "To Do" basket," Dani answered. "Then I'll call Macy and be done for the weekend."

Maureen nodded, "Then I won't feel guilty slipping out early."

"You can leave early any day you want," Dani assured her. "You do more than your fair share in this office. Soon, you'll be stuck with a trainee."

"This is the most interesting job I've ever held," Maureen told her. "You are more than just an attorney. You actually care."

"There are attorneys who don't care?" Dani questioned.

"I know some who only care about money," Maureen answered. "It's refreshing to work for someone who cares about people. Have a nice weekend." She grabbed her purse and headed out of the office.

Dani made her way to her desk, put the files in her basket, and reached for the phone to call Macy.

"McVannel," Macy answered her phone.

"Macy, it's Dani returning your call."

"Hey, Dani," Macy replied. "The woman you wanted me to check on is in the hospital."

"What happened?"

"Her husband beat her," Macy replied. "We have him in custody. He's being arraigned Monday afternoon."

"Does he have representation yet?"

"No, he will wait for court appointed."

"Is there any way you can get him arraigned last in the afternoon?" Dani asked.

Macy perked up, "Have you got a plan?"

"I'll be there in the afternoon and will represent him," she replied.

"Let me see what I can do," Macy told her. "I'll call you Monday morning."

"I'll talk to you then. Have a great weekend." Dani hung up the phone and pulled out the file Maureen had started on Ella's nephew-in-law. She placed it in her basket of things to do. Then she locked up the office and headed up the stairs to change for her evening with Brad and the children.

BRAD WAS USHERING the kids into wash up as Dani came down the stairs. He looked saying, "I hope you don't mind, I gave Ella the night off."

"I hope so, since we are going out," she retorted. "Do you have a destination in mind?"

"As a matter of fact," he began giving her a big grin, "I do, however I'm not telling you."

She laughed. "Of course, you're not. You've never been one to give away a secret."

"It's nice to know you remember," he answered as Teddy and Amy scurried down the hall toward them.

"Who has a secret?" Teddy asked.

"Mr. Brad," Dani answered checking his hands to be sure they were clean. Then she moved on to check Amy's hands. "All clean and ready to go."

"Let's get out of here then," Brad said ushering them out of the house toward his truck.

"What kind of secret, Mr. Brad?" Teddy asked as they settled into the back of the truck.

Brad put the truck in gear and answered, "I won't tell Miss Dani where we are going for dinner."

Teddy chuckled, "She will know when we get there."

Light hearted banter and laughter filled the truck as Brad drove into Willow Bend. He pulled into the parking lot of Benny's Burger Hut. Squeals of delight rang out from the back seat. Dani smiled knowing this was one of Brad's favorite hangouts when they had been kids. She wondered if he still frequented the place.

Moments later as they entered Brad was greeted by waitresses and patrons alike, Dani had her answer. Some things never changed. They found a table away from others so their presence would not bother anyone. They studied the menu together. Amy deciding on an order of chicken nuggets and fries. Teddy wanted whatever Mr. Brad was having. Dani decided on a BLT. Everyone had Pepsi to drink.

The kids were excited to be in a real restaurant. They were equally as excited to be able to choose for themselves what they wanted to eat. Dani smiled listening to them talk. Brad, too, was paying close attention to see what else the children had missed out on in their short lives.

Amy got all serious asking, "Miss Dani, what is a movie theater like?"

"Well, we buy our tickets, then get popcorn, candy, and pop," Dani started. "We give our tickets to the ticket taker, then go to the theater our movie is being shown in, and find seats. There will be some previews. They will turn off most of the lights so we can see the big screen. After the previews, we see the movie, then they turn the lights on and we leave."

"Can I sit by you?" she asked.

"Sure you can," Dani assured her.

"I'm sitting next to Mr. Brad," Teddy informed them.

Dinner arrived and conversation dulled as they ate. When they were done, Brad paid the bill and they ambled down the street to the theater. Much to Teddy's chagrin they chose to see *Brave*.

"Who wants to watch a movie about a girl?" he asked.

"You might find yourself surprised," Brad offered.

"If you say so," Teddy sulked.

Tickets, popcorn, candy, and pop purchased, they headed into the theater to find seats. They sat about midway up. Amy in first, followed by Dani, then Brad, with Teddy bringing up the rear. They hardly got seated when the lights dimmed and the previews began.

"Wow!" was all Teddy said after the first preview.

Amy was busy eating her popcorn. Dani and Brad enjoyed watching the children's delight in the previews. They could hardly wait until the main feature began.

At the end of the movie, Teddy began, "She was cool for a girl."

"She saved her mom," Amy replied. "Just like Teddy saved our mom."

Dani hugged her, "You are right."

They walked back to the truck, piled in and headed to Dani's. Teddy was quiet on the ride home and Amy fell asleep.

When they arrived, Brad said, "I'll carry Amy in."

"Thanks," Dani told him.

Teddy headed up the stairs ahead of everyone. He was already in bed by the time Brad and Dani got there with Amy. They tucked her in, then Teddy and left the two to their dreams.

Back downstairs, Dani asked, "Would you like a drink?"

"Not tonight, Sprite," Brad told her. He pulled her into his arms. "I'd forgotten how much fun going to the movies was."

"Me, too," she assured him.

He leaned in to kiss her and Dani melted into him. The passion between them sent electrical shock waves through her. She pulled away and just rested her head on his chest.

"I know, Sprite, I felt it, too," he said when he caught his breath. "I'm leaving before I get us both into trouble."

She let him go. He was out the door and down the steps to his truck before she even moved. *He was not the only one who could get them into trouble she thought.* Then she moved to lock the door and head up to bed.

CHAPTER TWENTY-FIVE

The sun was shining when Dani awoke the next morning. She heard the sounds of laughter from outside. *Oh, heavens, I must have overslept,* Dani thought as she leaped from her bed, grabbed her robe, and glanced at the clock. Seven forty-five! She shook her head and slowed down. She took her time getting dressed, used the bathroom to make herself presentable, and headed to the kitchen.

Ella looked up saying, "I fed the children and Mr. Brad an hour ago. He told me to let you sleep. Here's a cup of coffee and I have breakfast warming in the oven. Do you want to eat in the dining room?"

"No, here is fine," Dani replied taking the offered cup of coffee and moving to the table. "What was Brad doing here so early?"

"I believe he said he had to take some things into the tunnel," Ella told her. "The children must have heard his car, because he never got there."

"I see." Dani dug into her breakfast so she could join the others.

Amy saw her first, dropped her glove and came running, just as Brad tossed the ball to Teddy who gave it a good smack. It hit Amy square in the back and she dropped to the ground. Dani was at her side before she completely hit ground. Brad and Teddy came running.

"I'm so sorry," Teddy wailed. "I didn't know she was going to run across there. Is she dead?"

Brad took in the situation, "No, Teddy she's not dead. She got the wind knocked out of her."

Dani picked her up onto her lap. Amy coughed then began breathing normally. "You sure gave us a scare, Pumpkin."

It took a minute for Amy to answer, "What hit me?"

"I hit the baseball and it hit you," Teddy confessed. "But I didn't mean it."

"We know you didn't, Sport," Brad told him. "We just need to take Amy inside and let her rest for a bit. She'll be good as new after a rest."

"Sure she will," Dani affirmed. Even though she was a bit shaky on the idea herself.

Brad picked Amy up and they headed into the house. Dani sent Teddy upstairs to find Amy's favorite toys and a blanket, while she and Brad settled her on the sofa. When Teddy returned, Dani slipped into the kitchen to let Ella know what had happened. Ella set to work making Amy's favorite lunch.

Well, this crisis has been handled, Dani thought, *what next?* She went back to join the others.

BACK IN THE living room Brad had gone through some movies Dani purchased for the children to watch. They had settled on *Finding Nemo.* Amy was snuggled against Brad's side and Teddy was sprawled on the floor with a pillow. Brad motioned for Dani to join him and set the movie on play as soon as she was settled.

The movie was cute and held the children's attention. At some point about midway through the movie Ella came in with milk and cookies for the children coffee for Dani and Brad. She had been so silent it was almost as if it had appeared by magic. Dani thought the movie was cute. At the end Amy said, "I'm glad they found Nemo."

Brad suggested he take Teddy to some of his construction sites. He could show Teddy what he did and check on some sites he had neglected. As soon as they left, Amy went up to her room.

Dani took the dishes and left over cookies to the kitchen then decided to check on Amy. She found her fast asleep on her bed. So, Dani took the time to go over the three files in her office. Two were ready for sentencing according to plea agreements. She was going over the one for Rocky Evons. He was the one she would represent for the first time Monday afternoon. She wanted to be prepared for what she was up against.

He had done time for assault. This was not the first time he had been hauled in for domestic abuse. He was a three time loser. Dani thought she could squeeze him to a fifteen year plea with time off for good behavior. Meaning he would have to serve at least seven and a half. She could see Misty placed elsewhere in seven years. This would be a good opportunity to start her network.

She wandered to the kitchen around lunch time. Ella made her a sandwich and she ate in the kitchen. Amy was still sleeping. Something Dani normally would not worry about, but after getting the wind knocked out of her, it made Dani wonder if maybe they should have gone to the ER.

Left with time on her hands and not wanting to be far when Amy woke up, Dani curled up in her favorite chair to read a book. It was something she had not had time for since she moved in.

BRAD AND TEDDY came back just before dinner. Amy had slept most of the afternoon and was playing in her room. Dani was still curled up with her book.

"How was your day?" Dani asked looking up from her book.

Teddy piped up, "We saw lots of places. Mr. Brad called some of the site bosses and made them come see their mistakes."

"Site bosses, eh?" Dani looked over Teddy's head at Brad.

"I have site bosses, yes," Brad replied. "If Teddy ever wants to think about a job in construction, he needs to know the proper terms."

Dani smiled. She could see Brad had taken a shine to the children. "Well, Amy slept most of the day. I suspect she will be ready for dinner. Why don't you check on her when you wash up, Teddy?" she suggested.

Teddy raced for the stairs eager to tell Amy about his day. Brad crossed the room to Dani who stood to greet him. The kiss they shared would have lighted a dark room with all the passion if held.

When they separated Brad said, "I suppose I should wash up, too."

"Mhm," Dani moaned as she let him go. Smiling she went to get the kids for dinner.

ONCE DINNER WAS over, they played some board games until bed time. After the kids were tucked in, Dani helped Brad haul supplies to the tunnel. He set up the mini fridge so they could use it. He hoped to get to the beds in by Monday. He was building bunk beds and had a daybed to assemble. There was a microwave, stove top cooker, and a small convection oven. Dani had seen to it shelves were stocked with vegetables, fruit, tuna, and other non-perishables. She had planned to take Amy shopping today for bedding, towels, bath supplies, and paper products. Maybe they would go tomorrow.

They put things away and headed out toward the river. It was their favorite spot. The walked hand-in-hand to the end of the dock and sat down.

"I think I love this spot more than anyplace else," Dani sighed.

Brad slipped his arm around her as she dangled her bare feet in the water. "Mine, too."

"It's a good thing you own the property on the other side," she said. "I wouldn't want anyone spying on us."

He pulled her close and kissed her. Dani turned into him. As he broke the kiss he admitted, "Nope, no spies. This is our place."

"It will be until I start getting secret borders," Dani agreed.

Brad frowned, "I love you and the fact you want to help. I just don't want you getting hurt."

"I know," she said brushing a lock of hair from his forehead. "It's part of why I recruited you, Macy, and Eli. I'm protecting myself."

"Then you know there could be danger involved in this," Brad stated.

She nodded, "I've always known."

Brad said nothing just pulled her closer to him as if he could keep her safe forever. Knowing you cannot protect your loved ones all the time.

After a while Dani put her shoes back on and they walked to Brad's truck. Brad took her in his arms and kissed her as if it would be the last time. *He knew soon he would ask her to be his wife.* Breaking the kiss, he said, "See you in the morning."

"I'll have the coffee ready," she said smiling.

He got into the truck and drove away. Dani walked into the house, locked up, and climbed the stairs. She checked on the children before crawling into her own bed. Dreaming of the day Brad would not have to leave.

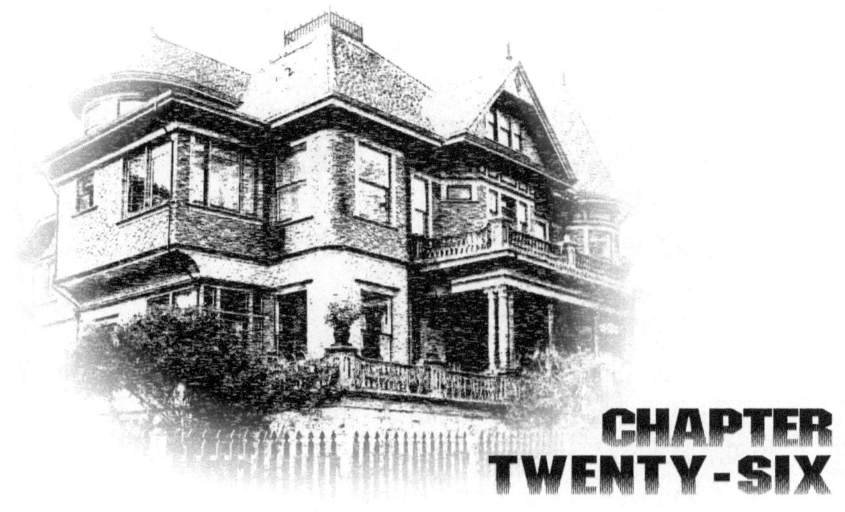

CHAPTER TWENTY-SIX

Dani and the kids were up early. They had eaten breakfast and were dressed for church when Teddy yelled, "Mr. Brad is here."

Amy and Dani came from the living room to the entry as Teddy opened the front door. Brad hustled everyone to his truck for a trip to church. At the church, Brad parked while Dani and the children waited for him before going into the sanctuary. They walked in and made their way about halfway down the aisle, the children sat between them. Amy spent her time before the service started watching people come in. Some stopped to say hello to Dani and Brad others just came in and found seats. Teddy studied the church bulletin as if he could read every word. As the organ stopped and the church bells rang, the minister stepped to the pulpit.

Midway through the service, the children were called to the front of the church for the children's sermon. Teddy took Amy's hand, walked with her to the front, and they sat with the other children. Brad slid closer to Dani and took her hand. After the sermon the children went to their respective Sunday school classes. Brad found it amusing the topic of the sermon was the Good Samaritan. While he said not a word, he gave Dani's hand a slight squeeze. She squeezed back in understanding.

They found the children after the service and spent some time talking to friends and neighbors before Brad went to get the truck and they headed home. Once at home, Dani sent the kids to change into play clothes.

"I think," Brad said, "I will check with Ella to see what she has planned for dinner today."

"Why?" Dani asked.

"Well," he started, "I thought maybe we'd go to my house and have a cookout. Let the kids explore a bit."

"Oh," she said.

"Did you want to do something else?"

Dani shook her head, "No, I thought maybe you'd be tired of us."

"Never," Brad feigned shock. "I love spending time with you and the kids."

Just then the kids in question scrambled down the stairs. Teddy asking, "What are we going to do today?"

"Wait for Miss Dani to change, then go to my house for a cookout," Brad told them.

Dani rolled her eyes and the children both looked at her with a hurry up expression on their faces. She headed up the stairs.

"Now while Miss Dani is getting ready, you two go get into the truck," Brad said. "I have to talk to Miss Ella."

The kids scampered outside as he headed to the kitchen. Ella looked up when he entered. "What do you need, Mr. Brad?" she asked.

"Have you got dinner ready?" he asked.

"All ready and in the basket," she smiled.

He planted a kiss on her aging cheek, "You're a dream. You and Sam enjoy the afternoon."

He picked up the basket she had packed for him and headed out to the truck. He tucked the basket in the back, made sure the kids were buckled in and waited for Dani.

When she came outside, he opened the door for her. As she climbed in he headed to his side to get in. They were soon on their way.

As they approached Brad's house, Amy asked, "Are your woods haunted Mr. Brad?"

"No, Amy," he told her. "Only the elves and fairies are allowed to live here with the woodland creatures and me."

She smiled knowing he was teasing her.

Teddy was looking at all the neat places wondering if there might be something magical to find. He asked, "Do you own all of this, Mr. Brad?"

"I do, Teddy," he answered. "Someday I will use this place just for hunting and getting away from everything."

"Cool," Teddy replied, then asked "Why would you want to get away?"

"Sometimes people need a break from their work. Lots of people go far away for vacations. I like it here," Brad explained.

Teddy pondered what he heard saying nothing.

As the children got out of the truck, Dani said, "You need to keep the house in sight at all times."

"Okay," they chorused scampering off.

Brad lifted the picnic hamper out of the back of the truck. Seeing this Dani smiled, "Got Ella to help you with this did you?"

He chuckled putting an arm around her waist as they walked, "Of course."

They went inside to check out the goodies Ella had packed. Then Brad fired up the grill. He could see the kids at the edge of the clearing. He was sure they would not wander too far into the woods before dinner. Later he would show them some of the paths he had explored. Maybe he could convince Dani to come along.

Inside, Dani was setting the table and peeking out the window to keep an eye on the kids. She was pleased to see they had not wandered into the woods. Maybe after dinner Brad would take them all exploring.

At the edge of the woods, Amy said to Teddy, "Can we go back now? The mosquitoes are biting me."

"I guess," Teddy really wanted to go into the woods. He turned and took Amy by the hand and they headed toward the house.

Dani was coming to call them in to wash up when she saw them coming toward the house. She raced out to see if something was wrong. Teddy had a scowl on his face.

Brad stopped her, "They are fine. I think they decided to wait until after dinner to explore farther."

"Oh, okay," she answered breathlessly.

"Give them a little space, Dani," Brad teased. "They are kids and want to explore." He winked, "We did."

"We were older when we went exploring," she reminded him.

"Maybe we can lead the explorations after dinner," he suggested.

"I'd like to," she smiled up at him. Then turned to watch as the children came up onto the deck. "You ready to get washed up for dinner?"

"Yeah," Teddy answered. "Mr. Brad, have you got something to take care of skeeter bites?"

"Sure, who needs it?"

"Amy, got herself all bit up," Teddy told him.

"Let me take the burgers off the grill and we'll get something. You two go get cleaned up."

Dani led the way in. She showed them where to wash up. Brad finished the burgers and brought them to the table. Then went to his medicine cabinet for Benadryl spray. He coated Amy and they went to have dinner.

They ate dinner and after dishes were done, sprayed everyone with bug spray and took off to hike in the woods. Amy not sure she liked the woods took Dani's hand and held on like it was a lifeline. Brad and Teddy explored everything the young boy's eyes found of interest. Part way down the path Dani and Amy found blackberries. Having thought ahead, they filled the small basket Dani had brought with her.

"These will make a great dessert," she told Amy.

"How are we going to cook them?" Amy asked.

"We're not," Dani assured her. "We are going to wash them and put them in bowls with milk and sugar."

"Okay," Amy said not sounding too enthused.

The two continued to pick until the guys came back. "Did you find anything interesting?" Dani asked.

"This could be an old Indian arrowhead," was Teddy's enthusiastic reply as he held out the arrowhead in his hand.

Dani looked at it, "Sure could be. How do you to feel about blackberries for dessert?"

"With milk and sugar," Brad added.

"Okay with me," Teddy said as he and Amy skipped ahead toward the house.

"They really are great kids," Brad commented. "How they have survived all they have been through is incredible."

"Kids are resilient and these two know their mom loves them," Dani answered.

"I suppose you're right," he conceded. "It makes what you are trying to do more personal for me."

She took his hand and squeezed it. He had just given his real approval and she knew it.

Inside Dani washed the berries and put them into bowls with milk and sugar. Everyone ate theirs and it was time to head home. They loaded the truck and climbed in.

"Thanks, Mr. Brad," Teddy said.

"I'm glad you enjoyed yourself," Brad responded. "Maybe we'll do it again sometime."

The rest of the ride was silent.

CHAPTER TWENTY-SEVEN

Dani was up early Monday morning, making sure the garden room had been turned into a bedroom and the bathroom across the hall was ready for Lizzy's arrival. She was gone before Maureen arrived, but left a detailed note sitting on her desk.

Arriving at the courthouse by eight-thirty, Dani went through the metal detectors and headed toward the courtroom. She had two men taking plea deals starting at nine. She was not surprised to see the DA Stamm already seated at the prosecution table. He smiled when he saw Dani enter.

"Miss Montgomery, pleased to see you this morning," he said reaching to shake her hand.

Dani shook his hand responding, "You, too, Mr. Stamm."

"I wish I had more attorneys like you," he said as he turned back to the files in front of him.

"Like me?" Dani questioned.

Stamm looked up from his papers, "Those who make my job easy by taking plea agreements."

"Oh, I don't always take pleas," Dani informed him.

"Two in the past week," he said, "it's a record even for me.

Dani made no comment and opened her brief case to take out the two plea agreements. The judge already had a copy and so did the district attorney. It was just a paper shuffling formality for her then she sat down. Stamm turned back to what he was doing as they waited for court to begin.

Not many people were in the gallery. The prisoners were in a room just off the court room and would be brought in one-by-one as their cases came up. Stamm had arranged for Dani's two clients to be first on the docket. The officer brought in Mr. Jackman and seated him next to Dani.

"Take a deep breath and answer the judge politely," Dani whispered. "It will be over in about five minutes."

Jackman just nodded affirmatively.

The bailiff entered and said, "All rise for the Honorable Judge James Beckett."

Everyone rose as the judge entered. Dani was not familiar with this judge. He was tall and distinguished looking with greying temples. He seated himself saying, "You may be seated. Bailiff, the first case."

"Windham County vs Theodore S. Jackman in a case of assault and battery."

The judge looked at the papers in front of him. "I see there has been a plea agreement."

Stamm spoke, "Yes, your Honor."

"Mr. Jackman, please rise."

He rose and Dani rose with him.

"You agreed to this?" Judge Beckett asked.

"Yes, sir."

"I see this is not the first time you have been in trouble. So saying, I am going to agree to the ten to fifteen year with one exception. You are to serve a minimum of ten years before you will be considered for parole."

Dani stifled a gasp.

"What the hell?" Jackman exploded. "This was a trick." He turned to Dani, "You bitch!"

The waiting officer had moved in to prevent him from taking a swing at his attorney. Spouting obscenities, he was led off to his cell.

Dani sat wondering what had just happened. She thought he might have to serve five to seven years of his sentence at the most.

"Ms. Montgomery, are you okay to continue?" asked Judge Beckett.

"Yes, your Honor," she replied regaining control.

Evan Hunter was brought in and seated next to Dani. She whispered, "Just be polite and answer calmly."

He nodded as the judge said, "Bailiff, next case."

"Windham County vs Evan Hunter on charges of assault and battery."

"I see again there has been a plea agreement," the judge stated.

Stamm again answered, "Yes, your Honor."

"Mr. Hunter, please rise," the judge said.

Dani rose with him. She was pretty sure she knew what the judge was going to say now.

"This is not the first time you have come before the court for this type of thing," the judge said.

"No, sir."

"I have read the plea agreement," the judge went on. "I concur with the exception of parole. You will not be considered for parole until after you have served the minimum ten years."

"You can't do that," Hunter bellowed.

"I can and I did," the judge said banging his gavel. "Escort Mr. Hunter from the room."

A stunned Evan Hunter was taken into custody. While the judge said, "We will take a ten minute recess."

Dani picked up her files and put them in her briefcase. Richard Stamm walked over to her.

"I'm sorry, Dani," he began. "I thought you knew about Judge Beckett."

"Knew what?"

"He always takes the minimum. They don't get out in half the time," he told her.

"It would have been nice to know when I was selling my clients down the river," she snipped. Taking her briefcase she pushed past the DA and left the courtroom.

DANI WAS STILL angry as she tossed her briefcase into the back seat. She took a deep breath to calm herself. It was good news she would be giving to Lizzy when she picked her up. Instead of just having five years to get on her feet and get out of town, she now had ten. Come to think of it so did Ms. Hunter. When she was calmer she started the car and headed to the hospital. It was time to reunite Lizzy with her children.

At the hospital, Dani made her way to Lizzy's room. A nurse was coming out as Dani went in. Lizzy was dressed and sitting in a wheelchair.

"Are you ready, Lizzy?" Dani asked.

"Miss Dani," Lizzy said a bit startled. "I didn't think you'd be here for at least an hour. Let me buzz the nurse's station." She reached for the buzzer on the bed.

In minutes the nurse who had passed Dani coming in returned. "I'm glad you are here. I know our patient is ready to go home," she said. "I have given her all her papers and the prescriptions she will need. If you pull around to the main doors, I'll bring her down and you can take her home."

"Thank you," Dani replied. "See you in a bit, Lizzy." She turned and walked out the door.

Five minutes later, Lizzy was in Dani's car and ready for the ride home. The nurse waved as they pulled out.

"I can't thank you enough for all you've done," Lizzy said.

"There is no need to thank me," Dani told her. "I know the kids will be excited to see you. I also have a bit of good news."

"Oh?"

"Your husband took a plea bargain and sentencing was this morning," Dani told her. "We had bargained him ten to twenty years in jail. I believed he would do five to seven years. The judge does not give parole until the minimum sentence has been served. Ted will have to serve ten years."

"What am I going to do?" Lizzy asked.

"I have my secretary ready to train you on how to run a legal office," Dani replied. "I will only have you working part-time to start and you will get a paycheck. You and the kids are welcome to stay on with me until we can find you a suitable job elsewhere."

"But won't he find me when he gets out?"

"No," Dani assured her. "We will get you a divorce, sole custody of the children, a job, a name change, and move you someplace where you can start fresh."

"You can do all those things?" Lizzy marveled.

"Yes, along with some friends of mine," Dani replied.

They rode the rest of the way in silence. Dani wondering what Lizzy was thinking and Lizzy wondering how lucky she was to have Dani in her life.

CHAPTER TWENTY-EIGHT

As they pulled into the driveway, Lizzy gasped. On the porch was a banner reading: WELCOME HOME MOM. Underneath it were the two smiling faces of her children and Brad.

"My beautiful babies," Lizzy whispered as tears of joy rolled down her cheeks.

Brad came to the passenger door when the car came to a stop. He opened the door, lifted Lizzy into his arms and carried her to the porch and her waiting children. He sat her in a rocking chair on the porch and stepped back.

"Mommy," the children said in unison as they hugged her from each side.

"Oh, my babies, I love you so much," Lizzy cried as she hugged them back. She found it hard to hug Teddy with her arm in a sling, but he did not seem to mind. She clung to Amy with her good arm.

Dani arrived on the porch in time to see the happy reunion. She had her phone out and was snapping pictures of the happy family.

"Shall we go inside?" she asked. "I think Ella has lunch for us."

"We already washed up, Miss Dani," Teddy informed her showing his hands for inspection.

Dani laughed as Brad leaned in to pick Lizzy up. The children scampered in ahead of everyone.

"We have a chariot awaiting you inside," he told her. Inside he set her gently in a wheel chair and guided it toward the dining room. Once there he helped her into a chair. Then joined everyone at the table.

Ella smiled as she served. The children kept up a running chatter to their mother about the things they had done.

"Mr. Sam has been teaching me about gardening, Mom," Teddy rattled. "And Mr. Brad has been teaching me to play baseball. We went to Mr. Brad's with Miss Dani for a picnic on Sunday after church, then we walked in the woods. Miss Dani and Amy picked blackberries and we had them with milk and sugar."

"Eat, Teddy," his mother admonished. "Give someone else a chance to talk."

Amy piped up with, "I don't get sick when I eat any more. Miss Dani took me to a nice doctor and got me some medicine. Miss Maureen let me be her 'ssistant one day and I got tired."

"Wonderful and after we eat I want to hear all about the things you've done," Lizzy said as she smiled at her children. She did not remember ever seeing them this animated. *What on earth have I put them through?*

"Mom, did anyone tell you, Miss Ella is the best cook?" Teddy asked.

"I would find out if you'd stop talking for a minute and let me eat," she chuckled.

Teddy went back to eating, so he would not make his mother angry. Silence reigned the rest of the meal.

When he was finished, Teddy asked, "May I be excused?"

"Me, too, please," Amy piped up.

Lizzy looked up in surprise saying, "Yes, you may." She watched in awe as her children quietly got up, pushed in their chairs, and took their dishes to the kitchen. "I don't know how you got them to do that, but I thank you. I guess I haven't been much of a mom." She hung her head as she finished her meal.

Dani was quick to say, "Lizzy, they are well behaved children who learned to be from you."

Lizzy looked up. "Are you sure?"

"I am," Dani assured her. "What they just did, they have been doing since they arrived here."

"Oh," Lizzy seemed puzzled. "I just remember Ted telling them to get out of his sight. I don't remember them taking their dishes, but they must have. I put them through a terrible ordeal staying with him, but I was so scared."

"It's over, Lizzy," Brad told her. "As soon as you get on your feet, we'll get you squared away. Would you like me to pick up some of your things and the kids from the apartment?"

"Would you?" she asked.

"Sure, but I need a key."

"In my things from the hospital is the key," she told him. "I'll get it."

Brad stood, "Let me help you get into the wheelchair and we'll get it together."

Brad helped Lizzy and Dani cleared the rest of the dishes. Once Lizzy was settled in the garden room, the kids went in to show her the things Miss Dani and Mr. Brad had given them.

Brad gave Dani a quick kiss and headed to the door. On his way out he said, "I'll be back for dinner with some of their belongings."

"Thanks, Brad," she told him as she headed toward her office.

She checked in with Maureen. "Hi, what did we have this morning?" Dani asked.

"A couple of calls on wills and a woman seeking a divorce lawyer," Maureen answered. "I take it the homecoming was a success?"

"In more ways than one," Dani answered. "No one warned me Judge Beckett took the lowest number of years as the minimum to be served. My clients both think I sold them up the river as they will be serving ten years before parole."

"Oh my, but won't it be better for the women involved?"

"It certainly will."

"Detective McVannel called and said she'd meet you outside the court house if you called her," Maureen said.

"Thanks, I'll call her on the road," Dani said as she emptied the morning files out her briefcase and picked up the file she would need in Rivers Edge. Then she was out the door for her next arraignment.

Once in her car, Dani pulled out her cell phone and pushed a button. She spoke clearly to Siri asking her to call Macy mobile.

A couple of rings later she heard, "McVannel."

"Macy, it's Dani. I should be there in twenty minutes," she said.

"I'll meet you in front of the courthouse, I want to talk to you before the arraignment," Macy replied.

"Sounds good," Dani said and hung up. She continued driving thinking about the upcoming arraignment.

DANI PULLED INTO the court parking lot and found a spot for her car. She stepped out, put on her suit jacket, picked up her brief-case, and locked her car. She headed for the court house keeping an eye out for Macy. She waved when she spotted her friend, sitting on the court house steps.

Macy rose and waved back. When Dani was close enough she said, "We need to find an empty conference room and talk."

"This sounds serious," Dani replied.

"Not as bad as it could be," Macy assured her.

They walked up the steps, went through the doors, and readied themselves for going through security. Once through, Macy led the way to the nearest conference room, she knocked on the door. When there was no response she opened it and they entered. Inside she locked the door.

"Macy, what on earth is wrong?" Dani was getting anxious.

"Do you have an alternate plan for Misty Evons if they release her husband?" Macy asked.

"What makes you think they will release him?" Dani wanted to know.

"I just don't know if there is enough to hold him and I'm worried in case he goes after her," Macy confessed.

"I can take her with me, but I have no idea where she lives," Dani said.

"Is your hideaway ready?"

Dani shook her head no, "Her aunt is my housekeeper. she could stay with them."

Macy paced, "I hate to dump this on you."

"Will you be in court?"

"You bet," Macy answered, "I want this scumbag held."

"Let's go see what we can do," Dani said heading to the door. "Which courtroom will we be in?"

"This way," Macy said walking to one the courtrooms.

Dani followed. She was a bit antsy now. All she had been given on Rocky Evons made it appear his case would be much like her last two, minus Judge Beckett. She took a deep breath, time would tell.

They took seats in the gallery and waited for Rocky Evons to be brought in for arraignment. There were several ahead of the one they were waiting for. All of them seemed to have attorneys and most were bound over for trial.

"Next case," the judge said.

The bailiff called the next case, "Rivers County vs Rocky Evons assault and battery with intent to kill."

Rocky Evons was brought in without an attorney. Things were looking up.

"Mr. Evons, do you have counsel?" the judge asked.

Dani stood, moving toward the front of the court room saying, "Danielle Montgomery for the defense your Honor."

"Excellent."

Dani stepped next to the defendant whispering, "I work pro bono."

Rocky nodded saying nothing.

"Ms. Stephens, how does the prosecution wish to proceed?" asked the judge.

"We wish to continue with the arraignment now the defendant has counsel," Sarah Stephens stated.

"Ms. Montgomery?"

"Please proceed your Honor," Dani replied.

"Mr. Evons, how do you plead to the charges against you?"

Rocky stood mute for a moment then said, "Not guilty."

"Prosecution on bail," the judge continued as if by rote.

Sarah shuffled some papers then said, "Prosecution requests remand. The defendant is a repeat offender, your Honor."

"Defense," again the judge sounded as if he were reading from a script.

"Defense concurs, your Honor," Dani said. "However we'd like to be on the books as wanting an early trial date."

Rocky looked at her like he wanted to strangle her, but to his credit said nothing.

"Remand it is, trial date for early next week," the judge responded bringing down his gavel.

As the guard came to collect Rocky, Dani leaned in to say, "Please take him to a conference room so we can discuss his case."

"Yes, Ma'am, I'll be standing right outside the room," the guard answered.

"Thank you." Dani gathered her things and walked from the court room. Macy stood and followed her out.

"Macy, I don't know when your prosecutor will be done, but I'd like to file my plea agreement with her before close of business today."

"You go talk your client into it and I'll watch for Sarah," Macy replied.

Dani headed to the conference room where she saw the guard standing outside. He opened the door, went in first, and left her closing the door behind him.

"Why didn't you ask for bail?" Rocky demanded.

"I have looked at your bank records Mr. Evons and knew you didn't have it," Dani replied.

"So, how are you going to get me off?" he wanted to know.

"I'm not," Dani replied. "We're going to ask for a plea agreement."

"The hell we are," Rocky shouted.

"Listen to me, Mr. Evons," Dani's calm voice seemed to reach him.

"Okay," he agreed.

"This is your third offense," Dani began. "The judge is going to want to throw away the key. If you change your plea to guilty, I think I can get the prosecution to go for a sentence of ten to fifteen years. Meaning you would serve between five and seven and be eligible for parole."

"If I go to trial, what do I get?" Rocky wanted to know.

"If you are found guilty, the maximum sentence which is twenty-five to life," Dani told him.

"What I gotta do?" Rocky wanted to know.

"Sign this paper," Dani said handing him paper and a pen, "I'll see the prosecutor gets it today and we should be able to get you on the docket by Monday. It also means you can get credit for the time you've already served."

"Sounds sweet, I'm in," Rocky said as he signed the paper in front of him.

Dani took the paper and pen, put them in her briefcase, walked to the door where she knocked and stood back. The guard entered.

"We are done here, thank you," she said and left the room.

Outside Macy was waiting for her with the prosecutor.

"Dani, this is Sarah Stephens, Sarah this is Dani Montgomery," Macy said making introductions.

The two women shook hands. "I have a plea agreement for you on Rocky Evons," Dani said.

"Let's go someplace and discuss it," Sarah said.

"Dani, call me when you are ready to leave," Macy said.

"Sure thing." Then she followed Sarah Stephens up the stairs to her office.

SARAH MOTIONED FOR Dani to take a seat, then she closed her door, and went around her desk to sit down. "Macy speaks very highly of you," she said.

"Thank you," Dani said. "I think the world of Macy."

Sarah shuffled some papers, "So, what is this plea agreement you have?"

Dani presented her with a signed copy of the plea agreement. Sarah took it and read through it.

She finished, put the papers down, and looked at Dani saying, "You are good."

"Thank you," Dani acknowledged. "How soon can we get him before a judge?"

"Well, it depends on the judge you want," Sarah said.

"Do you know Judge Beckett in Windham County?" Dani asked.

"Is he the one who takes the minimum years as the least the offender will do?"

"He is," Dani said nodding.

"We have one like him," Sarah confirmed. "I'll check the docket in the morning and see if we can get on it before the end of the week."

Dani stood handed Sarah her business card said, "Thanks, I appreciate it."

Sarah stood offered Dani her hand, the two shook and Dani left.

CHAPTER TWENTY-NINE

Dani waited until she left the building to call Macy. She was putting her jacket and briefcase in the car when Macy picked up.

"McVannel."

"Macy, it's Dani."

"How about meeting me at Dottie's Deli?" Macy suggested.

"Meet you there." Dani closed her phone and hopped into her car. She started up and made her way to the deli, found a place to park, and was getting out of her car when she spied Macy crossing the street on foot. She waved as she made her way to her friend.

"How did it go?" Macy asked.

"Hopefully we'll get scheduled for the end of this week," Dani said. "Are you still worried about Misty?

"I am." Macy said. "Rocky has three brawny brothers who will be checking in on her. When they hear bail was denied, they might smack her around."

"Nice bunch she married into," Dani's sarcasm was not lost on Macy.

"I have her in a safe house," Macy said. She slipped a piece of paper into Dani's hand. "Please pick her up on your way out of town."

"No problem," Dani said pocketing the slip of paper.

They were at the door by then, Macy opened it and led them to a booth near the rear. Dani looked at her surroundings.

"Did I just walk onto the set of *Happy Days?*" she asked taking in the dated décor.

Macy laughed, "It's rather quaint, but the food is good."

A waitress arrived at the table with glasses of water and menus. "Can I bring you ladies something to drink?"

"Iced tea with lemon for me," Macy replied.

"I'll have the same," Dani said.

"I'll be back with those, the special today is clipped with the inside the menus." She walked away.

"I don't know about you," Macy said. "I'm having the grilled chicken salad."

"Sounds wonderful," Dani agreed.

As they set their menus aside, Macy asked, "Do you and Brad have any plans for Wednesday night?"

"None I know of," Dani answered.

"Good, I want the two of you to come to my house for the last cookout of the season," Macy told her. "I want you to meet some of friends of ours."

"I'll ask him."

"It's not a work thing, Dani," Macy assured her. "JJ and Sally Mae are two people my partner Tom and I were assigned to protect a couple cases ago. Tom and his wife, Shannon will be there, too."

"Sounds like a good time," Dani agreed. "Do you need me to bring anything?"

"Only if you want to," Macy told her. "It's a bit last minute for you. The rest of us have been planning it for a week."

"I'm sure if I can't throw something together, Ella will."

"Ella, I almost forgot about her," Macy chuckled. "Does she still mutter under her breath?"

"Mostly when Brad and I are alone together," Dani confided. "It's a habit she's had for as long as I can remember."

The waitress arrived with drinks and took their orders. There was silence for a moment.

Macy broke it by asking, "Have you found out anything about the medical records I asked about?"

"As a matter of fact," Dani began, "I'm expecting a package from them when I return. If I think it'll help you, I'll bring it on Wednesday."

"Great."

"Can I take it things with you and Eli are still good?" Dani asked.

"Oh yes," was Macy's breathless answer.

"I'm so happy for you."

"Me, too," Macy's eyes sparkled as she smiled. "I hope things work out for you and Brad."

"We are learning about each other," Dani said. "I know more about him now than I ever did as a teen. I know he's good with kids and he wants his own."

"Are you getting serious?"

"I'm not sure what we're getting," Dani admitted.

The waitress arrived with their salads and conversation stopped momentarily as they began eating. When they finished, Dani commented, "This was really good."

"It usually is and this is later than I generally eat, so it's quieter."

Dani's look was filled with questions, "Do you frequent here often?"

"It's a cop hang-out for lunch," Macy answered laughing.

"I see." Dani's eyes twinkled mischievously.

Macy waved to the waitress, "Lunch is on me this time. I need to get back to work."

"Let me leave the tip," Dani said digging in her purse for her wallet.

The waitress brought the bill and took their plates. Dani left a generous tip while Macy paid the bill. The two walked out together. They hugged each other.

As they separated Macy reminded Dani, "Wednesday night seven sharp. Otherwise I hunt you down."

Dani laughed and waved to her friend as she made her way to her car.

ONCE IN THE car, Dani pulled the slip of paper out of her pocket and punched it into her GPS. Once it was ready, she started the car and followed the directions. It took her to an old farmhouse. Dani parked and walked to the back door. She was surprised to see the door answered by an elderly woman.

"Hello, you must be Macy's friend," the woman said pleasantly.

"Yes, I'm Dani Montgomery, I've come to pick up Misty Evons and take her to her aunt's."

"Do you want to come in?" the woman asked.

"I'd rather just pick up Misty and go if it's alright."

Misty answered from the top of the stairs, "Mrs. Appleton, it's okay. I've known Dani since I was a kid."

Mrs. Appleton turned, "If you're sure, dear."

Misty hugged the woman and said, "You've been so good to me. Thank you for everything."

"I'm here if you ever need me," Mrs. Appleton said hugging her back.

Turning to Dani, Misty said, "I don't have much I want to take, just this bag here."

"Let's go surprise Ella then," Dani said hugging Misty. *Lord, help me explain this to Ella. Misty had two shiners and her arm was in a sling.*

They got into Dani's car and drove off. Misty slid as far down in the seat as she could.

Thinking she might be uncomfortable Dani said, "Misty lean the seat back so it's in a reclining position."

Dani heard the motor on the seat as it moved lower. Misty sat up more in the seat and looked relieved.

"Do you want to talk about it?" she asked.

"Not really, Dani," Misty told her. "I've lived this nightmare much longer than I should have. I don't blame anyone but myself."

"I'm not passing blame or judgment, Misty Dani assured her.

"Never thought you would," was Misty's sullen response.

"Mrs. Appleton seems a little old to be assigned to guard duty," Dani said attempting to change the subject.

"Don't make me laugh," Misty said. "I have two cracked ribs. Mrs. Appleton, was doing a favor for Macy McVannel."

Confused Dani said, "I don't understand."

"About a year ago, McVannel and her partner solved the murder of her son. The case had grown cold because it was sixteen years old. Anyway, they ended up staying in the bunkhouse out back. It has some kind of panic room in it. McVannel knew I'd be safe because she'd call and warn us if we needed to be in the panic room. Some guy, JJ, lives in the bunkhouse and helps the old lady with the farm."

It all made sense to Dani now. She remembered hearing something about a big case involving Macy. "Wasn't the killer a police man?"

"Yeah, it was a huge scandal for a minute," Misty said. "Bad part was he had two more victims before he was caught."

"Wow, pretty sad," Dani said. "If you want, we are far enough out of Rivers Edge you could sit up again."

"If it's alright with you," Misty began, "I'd like to nap a bit."

"Sure," Dani said.

Misty closed her eyes and it was not long before Dani heard her even breathing. The rest of the ride to her house was silent.

CHAPTER THIRTY

When they arrived at Dani's she woke Misty. "I'm going to take you right to Ella and let her go for the evening."

"Thanks, Dani, I didn't mean to be so much trouble."

"It's my pleasure," Dani assured her. "I'm glad to get to see you."

They went to the house. Dani carrying the bag Misty had and straight to the kitchen. Ella looked up when they entered.

"Oh dear Lord!" Ella cried. "Child let me look at you." She walked to Misty with her arms outstretched. When she got closer she thought better of hugging her.

"Ella, you take Misty home," Dani said. "I can fix something for dinner."

Looking from one to the other, Ella said, "No need to Miss Dani. Miss Lizzy been in here giving me cooking lessons. Dinner is almost ready."

"Oh, okay," Dani stammered. "Well, you take the evening off and get Misty situated."

"Thank you, child." She took the bag Dani was holding then took Misty by the hand and led her out the back door.

DANI WENT TO her office. Maureen was there waiting.

"Looks like you've had quite a day," Maureen said.

"Feels like it, too," Dani told her.

"This packet came today," Maureen started. "I made a 10am appointment for you with a Mrs. Hendershot to make her will. Otherwise, everything is under control."

"Thanks, Maureen, you've been a trooper through all of this," Dani said. "I don't know what I would have done without you."

Maureen laughed, "This is much more exciting than anything I've done in the past ten years." She picked up her bag and made her way out the front door.

Dani went in to process the court cases she had handled today and to look at the packet on Chelsie Patton. She finished her follow-up on each case she had handled. Made a note to herself to call Mrs. Hunter and let her know her husband had been sentenced to a minimum of ten years. They would meet to get her set up with a job and identity as well as a ticket out of town.

She was about to start on the packet when Brad stuck his head in. "Are you going to work all night?" he asked.

Looking up with a smile on her face she replied, "No, I didn't realize it was time for dinner. Can I ask you something before we eat?'

"Sure."

"Have you got any plans for Wednesday night?"

"None I know of."

"We have been invited to Macy's for a cookout," she told him.

"Sounds grand, do we have to bring something?"

"Macy, said no, but I'll come up with something." She stood rounded her desk and walked into his arms. They had not had many minutes alone since the children moved in.

The sound of laughing children had them moving apart. Teddy and Amy bounded into Dani's office. "Miss Dani," they chorused. "Time for dinner."

She laughed, "Okay, where is your mom?"

"In the kitchen," Teddy answered. "She can't carry the hot stuff in her chair."

"Oh my, let's go help," Dani said leading the way out of her office.

Brad followed them all out, turned off the light, and closed the office doors. Then he headed for the kitchen.

Dani was surprised to see the table set. She followed the kids into the kitchen. Lizzy was there in her wheelchair with a huge salad in her lap. She was smiling.

"Miss Dani, if you could take the lasagna and garlic bread out of the oven we'll be ready to eat," she said.

"I'd be glad to," Dani said reaching for hot pads. She opened the oven and took the garlic bread out first. Seeing a platter sitting there she slid the bread onto it and set it on the counter. Making sure the oven was off, she reached in to get the lasagna. She set it on the top of the stove and shut the oven door.

"I'll carry the lasagna," Brad said entering the kitchen. "You just grab the garlic bread."

Dani turned and handed him the hot pads, then picked up the garlic bread and headed toward the dining room. She was pleased to note someone had put trivets on the table to hold the hot pan of lasagna.

"Hot stuff," Brad said as he came in with the lasagna. He set it on the trivets then sat down.

"Miss Dani, if you would dish up the salad," Lizzy began, "we can eat it while the lasagna has a few minutes to cool."

Dani began filling salad dishes and Lizzy passed them down the table. When Dani had filled enough to serve everyone, they began eating.

"This is a great salad, Lizzy," Brad said.

"It is my grandmother's recipe, so is the lasagna."

"Do you have other recipes from her?" Dani asked.

"I have them all in my head," Lizzy answered. "Cooking is something I've always wanted to do."

"Great," Dani replied.

Brad cut and dished out the lasagna. Lizzy passed the garlic bread around and they began eating. For dessert, Lizzy sent Teddy to the kitchen for a bowl of mini zeppoles…a concoction of pizza dough fried in mini balls and dusted with confectioners' sugar. It was the rave of the evening.

"You can make it and drizzle honey or chocolate, too," Lizzy told them. "Since I was making an Italian dinner I thought I'd make an Italian dessert."

"Lizzy, I'm going to get fat if you keep feeding us like this," Dani moaned.

"I will try Greek next time," Lizzy assured her.

Brad and Dani cleaned up the dishes, putting leftovers in the refrigerator, and snatching extra desserts. Lizzy and the children went to her room. She read them a story then Dani appeared to take them to bed.

Once the kids were tucked in, Brad and Dani settled on the sofa in her living room.

"It's going to be winter soon," Dani said. "How will we get women and children to the safe house?"

"Your cavern hideout?" Brad asked. "We will find a way."

She snuggled into him, "I like this."

He circled his arm around her and pulled her in for a kiss. When he let her go he said, "Me, too."

A while later, Brad shifted and moved Dani out of his arms. "As much as I enjoy this, I need to go home." He stood and stretched.

Dani stood beside him and they walked to her front door. "Tell me one day you won't be leaving me."

Brad pulled her in to kiss her goodnight saying, "One day I won't be leaving you." Then his lips met hers before she could say a word. "Night, Sprite," he said when he let her go. He opened the door and was gone.

Dani locked the door and headed for her office. She really wanted to see what was in the file on Chelsie Patton. She hoped it would be of some use to Macy. She flipped on the lights and went to her desk.

Sitting at her desk she picked up the envelope and took out the contents. She started with the letter from the private facility Chelsie had been sent to.

Dear Ms. Montgomery,

We are sorry to hear Chelsie has had a relapse. We had hoped she finally put all of this behind her.

Chelsie came to us after a summer camp experience. I've enclosed a photo of her at the time. We make a practice of photographing all our young patients. She was quite overweight and lacked self-confidence. She had been picked on mercilessly at the summer camp.

It led to a total emotional breakdown. She was with us for six months before we felt she could be out in the world and not harm herself. We kept her another two months as we oriented her back into the real world.

Once you have read the transcripts of her sessions and the medical treatment she received if you still have questions, please call me at 510-555-9998.

Sincerely,
Dr. Michael Jonas,
Loving Care Pediatrics Center

Dani pondered the letter for a few minutes then picked up the intake form on Chelsie. The photo showed a pre-teen with weight issues and dark hair. *I thought Macy said this girl was a blonde. She appeared to have a nice complexion.* Dani thought her eyes looked empty. *Almost as if she wasn't there. Like her body was just a shell on autopilot.*

According to the report, Chelsie was put on a diet and exercise routine. She had daily sessions with a counselor and in group. To begin with she had not responded. She ate what was put in front of her and went through the motions of calisthenics. Her weight started to drop, but she was still not responding.

In a staff meeting where they discussed patient care, improvement, and issues someone suggested she learn to meditate. Chelsie responded to yoga and meditation. She would spend hours near a brook on the property listening to her inner self. She could be seen doing yoga and sitting in the lotus position meditating.

While staff still could not get her to talk, she was steadily losing weight and cooperating. She was not talking to anyone. Not in group or with her counselor one-on-one. Stumped someone suggested maybe she should keep a journal. A notebook and pen were provided for her and she was told she needed to put her feelings in it for her next individual session.

Finally compliance. Chelsie started out by writing her feelings while doing yoga or meditating. She commented on how she felt much better about herself having lost what she termed "baby" weight.

One entry from the early days read like this: *I am by the babbling brook. It is a soothing sound. I breathe in the freshness of the water. I become the water floating way. I am weightless. The yoga makes my muscles feel alive. Like I am sending electrodes to each nerve. Never have I felt like this before. When I meditate, my mind empties and I see the future. My future, is bright full of love. Rich in all things. I will have it all.*

It seemed to Dani like she was reciting a litany to keep her true feelings to herself. She could not see where this was headway of any kind. Whatever ailed Chelsie Patton was deep-seeded. Dani hoped there would be something of more help in the file. For now she set it aside, turned off the light, and headed for her bed. She would finish the file in the morning.

Dani thought she was early when she entered the kitchen at seven the next morning. She was shocked to see the children dressed and getting ready to take food to the dining room. Ella and Lizzy were supervising.

"Miss Dani, breakfast is being served in the dining room," Amy informed her as she carried a dish of muffins through the door.

Dani said nothing, just followed the children. Teddy had a plate of bacon and Lizzy was navigating her way in her wheelchair balancing a covered plate. Ella brought up the rear with a pan of something and the coffee pot. They set everything on the buffet.

"Go ahead, Miss Dani," Teddy said proudly.

She picked up a plate, put some bacon, a muffin, some eggs, and butter on her plate. She set it on the table and sat down. Ella poured her coffee and left the room. Teddy helped Amy fill her plate, then filled his own.

"Mom, do you want me to help you?" he asked.

"No, I'm fine. Thank you, Son," she said smiling.

"This is wonderful," Dani said when they were all seated. "Lizzy, you are not required to do the cooking."

"It is the least I can do," Lizzy answered. "Besides, someday I'd like to have my own little restaurant."

"Really," Dani said.

"It's always been a dream of mine," she answered. "I love cooking and most people don't get home cooking when they eat out."

"Have you thought of a name for it?" Dani wanted to know.

"No," Lizzy answered. "It's just a dream."

"Maybe not," Dani said. "Let me make a couple calls. We can talk later this afternoon."

"Okay," she answered.

Dani noticed she seemed to have lost her spark. But she knew one of the things Lizzy needed was a steady income and the ability to support herself and her children. She dropped the subject for now.

ONCE IN HER office, Dani pulled the papers she would need to create a will for her next client. She set it to the side and picked up the Chelsie Patton file. She was sure it was going to cause more questions than it was going to give answers.

The next was a notation from the counselor. It read:

I find Chelsie to be changing before my eyes, even though she still does not talk to me or participate in group. She gives the impression she is above the rest. Her problems overwhelm her, but she is not willing to share them and make herself vulnerable to others. I believe I will look into her family background, maybe there is something hidden there.

Dani found this puzzling. What did Chelsie have to hide? What made her think she was better than the others? She quickly jotted the questions down, she and Macy were going to have to sit down and talk about this. Maybe they should include Macy's partner and the assistant district attorney who would be prosecuting this case. She shook her head and read on.

Six months into the program a second photo was taken. The difference between the two was extraordinary. Chelsie had lost probably fifty pounds. She was slender and willowy in the new photo. The thing Dani saw which troubled her was the emptiness in her eyes. They remained unchanged from the first photo. Whatever had happened to this girl was traumatic. Dani made a note to see if she could get a hold of photos of Chelsie before the age of twelve. She wanted to know just when the change took place. Dani suspected it was before the summer camp.

She looked up smiling as she heard Maureen come in. Maureen wanted to know if Dani needed her to do anything.

"Have a seat, Maureen," Dani said gesturing to one of the chairs in front of her desk. She turned her chair, stood, picked up her cup, poured another cup of coffee and one for Maureen. Handing Maureen her coffee, Dani sat back down. "I have some news," she began. "I mistakenly thought you would be training Lizzy to run a law office."

Maureen sipped her coffee, "Is she going to learn something else?"

"It seems she has a skill and a dream," Dani said. "She's been taking over the kitchen and cooking meals since dinner last night. I must admit, she's good. It seems she has always wanted a small restaurant and bakery with home cooking like her grandmother used to do."

"How wonderful," Maureen said with sincerity. "How can we help?"

"I'm not sure yet," Dani told her, "But if she comes to you and wants you to type up recipes for her will you do it?"

"Of course," Maureen agreed," who knows she might end up being famous."

"Who is coming in this morning for a will?" Dani asked putting them back on track.

Maureen chuckled as she answered, "Mrs. Agatha Hendershot, I believe she is a widow."

"It will be interesting, I'm sure," Dani agreed. "I'm going back to the package you received yesterday. It, too, is very interesting in a disturbing kind of way."

Maureen stood, taking her coffee with her, "I'll let you get to it." She went to her desk just as the phone started ringing. "Montgomery Law Office, how may I help you?"

Dani picked up the file again she knew Maureen could handle most things. She wanted to dig deeper into this disturbed child. More reports read much as the previous ones. Finally she hit on a follow-up from the counselor.

It seems Mrs. Patton inherited money from her grandmother which made the family a bit more affluent than they had been. There is a trust fund for Chelsie when she turns twenty-five. She is an only child the mother had lost a child when Chelsie was three. There had been no other pregnancies. Mr. Patton had invented something and sold it for millions.

This was when they moved to Rivers Edge. Chelsie was six and had grown up believing she was royalty.

No wonder she thinks she is superior to others, she has been spoiled all her life. First, because she was an only child and then because she is a trust fund baby. But, to Dani it did not explain the emptiness in her eyes. The total lack of human emotion. *There was something she was missing.*

Maureen came to the door and knocked. Dani looked up and could see an elderly woman behind her, "Mrs. Hendershot is here."

"Come in, Mrs. Hendershot," Dani said putting aside the Patton file and coming around her desk to greet her client. "I'm Dani Montgomery."

Mrs. Hendershot came in and Maureen closed the door on her way out. "Please, have a seat. Can I get you some coffee?" Dani indicated the chair in front of her desk.

"No, thank you," Mrs. Hendershot said. "This is not a social call."

Dani retreated behind her desk, "I understand. What is it you would like me to do?"

"I am not getting any younger," she began. "I need to get my affairs in order which includes making a will. I have two grandsons already fighting with each other to see who can do the most for me and win my money."

"Have you decided how you want your estate divided?" Dani asked. She had already noted there were two heirs.

"I want each of them to inherit ten thousand dollars not a dime more and the rest of my estate to go to the local chapter of Paws Rescue," she said. "They save abandoned dogs."

Dani wrote this down then asked, "How much is your estate worth?"

"Approximately four million dollars," she said. "Of course, you will need to see to the sale of my house and belongings. I don't want those two scalawags to loot the property."

"I will arrange for an estate sale when the time comes," Dani assured her. "Are there any other relatives who might contest the will or be included?"

"No, the boys are the last of my relatives living," Mrs. Hendershot told her. "They are lazy and believe they will profit from my death. I plan to teach them nothing is free."

"Absolutely," Dani agreed. "I'll draw this up. You tell me when you'd like to come back and sign it."

"I'd like to come back later today, if you don't mind," she said.

"Is three o'clock a good time?" Dani asked.

Mrs. Hendershot stood, "I will be here at three sharp." Then she left the room.

Dani had no time to stand and see the woman out. She was a bit shell-shocked. Maureen came in.

"Is everything okay?" she asked.

"I'm not sure," Dani answered. "Mrs. Hendershot will be back at three to sign her will. Did she happen to give you the names of her two grandsons?"

"She did when she called," Maureen said. "Just give me the notes and I will insert their names."

Dani handed her the notepad and Maureen went off to get the will typed and ready for signature. She suspected Mrs. Hendershot would be signing it at one minute after three.

LIZZY ROLLED IN with the morning break treat. She left a small plate on Maureen's desk and rolled her chair to Dani's office. She knocked on the door frame. Dani looked up and said, "Come in, Lizzy. You don't need to knock."

"Miss Ella told me she brings you and Miss Maureen a morning snack so I thought I'd make them this morning," she explained coming in with the second plate.

Dani came around her desk to take the plate from Lizzy, "This looks wonderful," she said as she looked at the treats on the plate. She spied cookies, brownies, and some other kind of pastry. "You didn't need to go to so much trouble."

"It was no trouble," Lizzy replied, "and we have plenty for dessert." She turned to roll out then hesitated and asked, "Do you really think I could own a restaurant and bakery?"

"I'll see what I can do," Dani said smiling as she watched the smile bloom on Lizzy's face.

Lizzy rolled out of the office and Dani thought she heard her humming. She sat at her desk and opened the Chelsie Patton file again.

CHAPTER THIRTY-TWO

Dani was deep in the Chelsie Patton file when she heard a knock on the door. Looking up she smiled at Amy.

"Miss Dani, are you going to come to lunch?" Amy asked.

Looking at the clock she saw it was quarter to one and lunch was usually served at twelve-thirty. "I'm coming right now," she answered putting the papers she was reading in the file.

Together they made their way to the dining room. Ella was serving. Maureen chose to take her lunch with Ella.

"Oh this looks good," Dani began. "I'm sorry to have kept you waiting."

Lizzy grinned, "It's okay we are not starving."

"So who cooked today?" Dani wanted to know.

"Actually, Miss Ella shared one of her recipes with me," Lizzy answered. "We are thinking of writing our recipes down and putting them in a book."

"Excellent idea!" Dani beamed. "You can sell them in the bakery and restaurant you want to open."

"We have to figure out how to divide the profits," Lizzy said. "I don't want to cheat Miss Ella."

Ella was smiling as she made her way into the kitchen. *At least she was not feeling threatened in the kitchen*, Dani thought.

Lunch passed quickly. The children were very proud of their mother and her cooking abilities. They delighted in asking her about it. Dani enjoyed listening to them finding out about this new side of her.

She went back to her office looking forward to reading more on Chelsie Patton. She had an idea to help both the police and the prosecutor on this case. Still there was much more reading to be done before she could present it to them.

Dani heard Maureen answer the phone, then hers rang, "Yes?"

"It's Brad on line one," Maureen said.

"Thank you," she answered then switched to line one, "Brad, this a surprise."

Dani looked up hearing her door close. Maureen thinking she needed privacy. Dani smiled.

"I hate to be a drag, but I can't make dinner tonight," Brad apologized.

"Are you still planning to go to the cookout with me tomorrow?" she asked.

"Wouldn't miss it, but I need to get this project I'm on done so I can," he answered.

"Don't overwork. I'll see you tomorrow."

Brad sighed, "I love you, Dani."

"I love you, too." Then she hung up the phone. She rose and opened the door to her office. She was surprised to see Misty in the office.

"Dani, can we talk?" Misty asked.

"Certainly, come on in," Dani replied standing aside so Misty could enter. Misty walked in and sat in one of the chairs facing Dani's desk.

After shutting the door, Dani walked to her desk, "You look a bit better."

"How I look is not the problem," Misty told her. "I need to get out of here before Rocky's brothers come looking for me."

"Okay," Dani told her, "How soon do you want to leave?"

"Tomorrow if possible," Misty told her.

"What name do you want to go by?" Dani asked. "I will get you new papers with a new identity."

"I am a beautician," Misty said. "How will I get my credentials?"

"Let me worry about it," Dani said.

"Okay, can I be Michelle?"

"Do you have a last name picked out?" Dani asked.

"No, as long as it's not Evons."

"What's your maiden name?" was the next question from Dani.

"Wicks."

"How does Michelle West sound?" Dani asked.

"I could get used to it."

"I'll make some calls and get on it," Dani assured her. "It might take a couple of days, but I have someplace you can stay if you would feel safer."

"If you have a safe house somewhere, I'm ready to go."

"Go tell your Aunt," Dani said. "Then pick up whatever belongings you have at her house and come back here."

"Okay." Misty got up to leave she turned when she opened the door, "Thanks, Dani."

"No problem."

Misty headed for the kitchen.

DANI WENT TO her door, "Maureen, I need to see you." She then went back to her desk.

Maureen entered and closed the door, "What do you need, Miss Dani?"

"I need you to draw up divorce papers for Misty Evons," Dani told her. "She will be going into the chamber room this afternoon."

"Sounds like she is still in danger," Maureen replied. "I will get right on it." She rose, opened the door, went to her desk took out the papers necessary to file for divorce.

Dani returned to the Chelsie Patton file. Reading it only confirmed something had happened to the girl before she arrived at the camp and what happened at camp sent her over the edge.

Counselor narrative:

Having worked with Chelsie for several months, I see no real improvement. She continues to be withdrawn. Her silence in group has forced me to remove her from it. She seems pleased by this, as if she is above the other girls in the group.

She is still making journal entries, but to me they seem trite. They are not a release of her pent-up anxiety. I have three months to sort her out as her time here will be up. Her parents visit, however I do not see active communication between them. I am frustrated, at a loss for what to do. Here is her latest journal entry.

Today while in group I refused to talk. I do not care about the petty issues these girls have. They have no clue how cruel the world is. The counselor is finally taking me out of group. I am better than these girls.

I enjoy my time at the brook. It is soothing to listen to when I meditate. I am glad I learned how to do this. I can leave myself and be one with nature. I can rise above all others. The yoga has toned my body and I have become a goddess. All is good in my world. I can hardly wait to break out of this place.

How is this girl a goddess? What is she trying to bury? I cannot seem to break through and I fear how this will end for her down the road.

Dani wanted to know what had happened to this girl. She learned to cope and hide her emotions. She became a manipulative monster by the time she was seventeen. Early pictures would tell when the change took place. She would also like to see current photos of the girl to see if the dead look is still in her eyes. Something went seriously wrong in this child's life. Something which might explain her actions or not.

She put the file away and looked at the clock Mrs. Hendershot was due any minute. She needed to round up Ella to sign as a witness to the will. Dani headed toward the kitchen.

"Ella, can you witness a will for me?" she asked entering the kitchen. She stopped short looking at the faces gathered there. Ella was crying, Lizzy and the children were trying to console her. "What has happened?" Dani wanted to know.

"Miss Dani," Lizzy began. "Let me witness the will." She turned her chair and wheeled toward where Dani was standing inside the door.

"Sure, fine," Dani responded holding the door so Lizzy could get through.

They made their way to Dani's office just as Mrs. Hendershot arrived.

"Good, I like people who are prompt," she replied.

They entered the office and proceeded to Dani's office. "Here is the document," Dani said handing it to her. "Would you like a minute to read it over?"

"I believe you are capable of following my instructions," Mrs. Hendershot replied.

"Then let me bring in the witnesses," Dani said going to the door and asking Maureen and Lizzy to come in.

Mrs. Hendershot signed her will, then Maureen and Lizzy signed it, finally Dani signed it. Maureen took the will and made two copies. The original would be filed with the court when she died and a copy would remain in the office. Mrs. Hendershot would get a copy.

When the copies were dispersed, Mrs. Hendershot said, "Thank you all." She turned to Maureen to pay her bill.

"Lizzy, will you stay please?" Dani asked.

Lizzy came toward Dani's desk. "I know you want to know about Miss Ella. She's upset about her niece."

"I thought as much," Dani replied. "I think if I talk to her I can set her mind at ease."

"Send the children to my room," Lizzy said.

Both women left the office. Lizzy for her room and Dani for the kitchen.

Dani found the kids eating cookies and Ella working on dinner. "Kids, your mom wants to see you in her room. Why don't you take her a cookie?"

"But, Miss Dani, we are only supposed to eat in the kitchen," Teddy protested.

"I think she'll give you a pass this time," Dani assured him.

The two kids scampered out and down the hall.

"You are spoiling those children, Miss Dani," Ella admonished.

"It's the least I can do," Dani answered with a smile. "Ella, Misty is not leaving today."

Ella looked up, "She told me she was."

"She is only leaving your house," Dani said. "She doesn't want to put you and Sam in danger. I am putting her in the chamber room until we can move her safely out of town."

Wiping her hands the tears flowed down Ella's cheeks. She came around the corner and hugged Dani. "Thank you, so much."

Dani hugged the woman back, "I'd have told you if she was leaving."

"I'm so scared for her," Ella admitted.

Dani broke the hug, "Misty knows how to take care of herself. She was afraid of being a failure and scared of Rocky and his brothers. Not anymore."

Ella wiped her eyes with her apron. "I'm so glad she has you in her corner."

Dani smiled, "I need to get back to work. Misty will be filing for divorce today. It's her first step to freedom."

"Shoo, get on out of here then," Ella said going back to her baking.

Chuckling because she knew things in her household were once again all right, Dani went back to her office.

"Maureen, when Misty comes back have her come right in and bring the divorce papers," Dani said returning to her desk and the Chelsie Patton file.

She pulled out her note pad and wrote, *need photos from one year to age 12 before camp, need to learn if she still journals, looking for a change in her personality and facial expression. When did her eyes become blank? What is she hiding?* Then she began to read in the file again.

Counselor last entry:

I have made no headway with Chelsie. She is as shut off as the day she arrived. She says nothing in counseling sessions. She continues to do yoga and meditate near the brook. She eats alone. She interacts with no one. She has been weaned off all meds yet there is no change. I can see a metamorphosis in her body. She has lost the baby weight and toned herself with yoga. I suspect the yoga and meditation will be part of her daily regime. Especially if she can find a place near water. I just fear one day she will no longer be able to hold in whatever secret she has.

Chelsie's last entry she shared with me:

Tomorrow is freedom day. I get to go live in the world. A world I will make a difference in. Never again will anyone look down on or get the best of Chelsie Patton. I am superior to those who would try to bring me down. I will show them who I am. Tomorrow is the first day of the rest of my life. And what a glorious life it will be.

Dani, too wondered if holding in her fears had caused the young girl to do things she never would have prior to her trauma. Tomorrow night was going to be interesting if she had a chance to talk to Macy about the case.

CHAPTER THIRTY-THREE

Misty arrived just before dinner. She carried a small bag as she entered Dani's office. "I think Dani wanted to see me," she told Maureen.

"You can go right in. She's expecting you," Maureen told her.

She left her bag on a chair and walked into Dani's office. Dani looked up from the papers in front of her and said, "Will you close the door please?"

Misty closed the door and took a seat in front of Dani's desk. "What do I need to sign to disappear?"

"For starters, you need to sign these divorce papers," Dani told her. "You will have to appear in court one time to get them through. Since you and Rocky have no children and you are not asking for any of the communal assets, there should be no problem. I have arranged for you to appear in court here tomorrow."

"I thought I was making a getaway tonight," Misty protested.

"There are still more contacts I have to make to get your identification, your next destination, and some cash to get you started," Dani explained. "I also don't want Rocky getting out at some point in the future and coming after you because you are still his wife. I want you to be free to meet and marry a nice man."

"Guess I didn't think about all those things. Sorry, Dani."

"No problem. Tonight you are having dinner with Lizzy, her children, and me. Lizzy is about to make the same journey you are with her children," Dani said. "My job is to get some of you started and to house others. I have a safe house no one knows about. You will be its first occupant, so I need you to leave me a list of what's missing." Dani chuckled.

"Okay, I guess."

"It will be okay in the long run," Dani assured her. Then she went over the divorce papers and Misty signed them. Dani placed them in a file on her desk and they rose together. "I'm going to miss you. You can write to the law office, so I can let Ella know how you are doing. Get a post office box for replies. They will come only from me. So, get it in a neighboring town from where you live. Have a regular mailbox for you daily stuff. I can never know where you are." Dani hugged her childhood friend and Misty hugged her back.

DINNER WAS LIVELY. Lizzy prepared a stew from last night's leftovers which had everyone asking for seconds. She made dumplings and of course there were all the cookies and goodies she made earlier for dessert.

Misty looked at Lizzy after the children had gone off to play, "What are you going to do when you leave here?"

"I'm hoping to open my own bakery and restaurant," Lizzy told her.

"You'll be good at it."

Dani smiled at the two women who were refugees of the spousal war. *How did good women get taken in by these creeps?* She went about clearing the table while the two women talked.

"Can I pry and ask how you ended up so battered?" Misty asked.

"Sure, but I'm going to ask you the same thing," Lizzy said laughing. "It started out with my husband telling me I was totally incompetent as a wife. My housekeeping didn't measure up to his standards, my food was awful and never on time. He didn't start hitting me until Amy was born. She was a colicky baby and cried a lot. I put up with it as long as he didn't hit the kids. I taught Teddy when he was four to dial 9-1-1. I hate to think how many times he's had to call." Lizzy shook her head. "What was I thinking to stay?"

"I understand," Misty told her. "Rocky never hit me unless he was drunk. Of course, he was always telling me I was worthless. He made me quit work as a hair stylist. He didn't want me to have my own money. I was a fool."

"We are a pair of fools," Lizzy agreed.

Dani entered just in time to hear the last comment, "Neither of you is a fool. You were caught up with men who are good at manipulation."

"Look at us," Misty could barely contain her anger. "We had to get the shit kicked out of us to realize we were in bad relationships. I'm betting this is not the first time Lizzy has been beaten. I know it's not mine."

"She's right, Miss Dani," Lizzy's calming voice cut in. "I cannot count the number of times I took a beating. Why did I stay?"

"There are a multitude of reasons why women stay with men who abuse them," Dani told them. "Not one of them is any better than another, some women think this is how it's supposed to be. There isn't an easy answer."

"Stupidity," Misty said. "There is no excuse for it. No reason I should have stayed."

Dani frowned, "I wouldn't call either of you stupid. But sitting here arguing about it isn't going to change things."

"Agreed," Lizzy said. "I should go read a bedtime story to my kids. Miss Dani are you still going to tuck them in?"

"In about an hour, I'll come get them."

"Great." Lizzy whirled her wheelchair toward the door and down the hall to her bedroom.

"Let's go get your bag," Dani said standing up and heading to the office.

Misty followed. Once there, Dani began closing up the office as Misty picked up her bag. Then as Dani shut-off the light and closed the door, she said, "Follow me."

The two friends went up the stairs where Dani opened the closet door and stepped in. Not knowing what to expect, Misty followed her closing the door. Dani already opened the passage door and stepped inside. Still not asking questions, Misty followed. She heard the door close behind her. Dani continued down the well-lit winding hallway until it opened into a larger room.

"What is this place?" Misty asked.

"It is a sanctuary for abused women on their way to freedom."

"Wow, is all I can say."

"There is food in the fridge and the cupboards. You can cook whatever suits you. The room is sound proof, so no one will know you are here. Cable is connected to the TV and there are a ton of videos. The bathroom is fully functional, so make yourself at home," Dani hugged her. "I suspect Ella will be down to see you at some time tomorrow."

"I can't thank you enough, Dani."

"Yes, you can. Be a successful hair stylist, find a good man, and have a great life."

Dani turned and made her way up the hallway to the linen closet. Misty took in her surroundings and marveled at the task her friend had taken on. The bunk beds were made and the daybed was ready to use. The room was colorful and cheery. The flat screen TV hung on the wall. There was a sink, dishes, paper plates, silverware, pots and pans, everything to stay for an extended period of time. She even found board games, cards, books, and puzzles. This was going to be okay.

Misty used the bathroom, got ready for bed, found a good book and crawled in.

CHAPTER
THIRTY-FOUR

Dani returned to the house and went to collect the children and tuck them into bed. Lizzy was just finishing the bedtime story. Amy was already asleep.

Lizzy whispered, "Just leave her here tonight."

Dani nodded and motioned for Teddy to come along. He slid out of bed and took her hand.

On the way upstairs Teddy said, "Did you know we only had one bed to sleep in at our apartment?"

"No, Teddy, I didn't."

"The nights he didn't beat her too bad, Mom came in and slept with us. I think it made her feel safe."

Dani smiled, "I'll bet it did."

"I like having my own bed," he told her. "Do you think in our next place I can get my own room?"

"You know, I bet you probably can." She tucked him into bed and turned out the lights.

"Thanks, Miss Dani, for saving us."

"I'm glad I could help." Closing the door she walked to her own room. She wondered, *What might have happened to them if I hadn't stepped in? Dead mother and shipped into foster care. Products of a sys-*

188

tem gone wrong. Shaking the thoughts away she slipped into night clothes and into her bed.

She had always felt home was a safe place. She had her parents for the first sixteen years. They had been her anchor. Her grandparents had stepped in when she lost her parents. They had given her sanctuary in their home. Unlike Teddy and Amy who had known only violence and one parent who tried to step between it and them. She hoped they would heal.

Her mind just couldn't shut down. *I hope Misty is finding what she needs and gets a good night's sleep. I know Ella is happy she is safe. I wonder what their lives will be like? Misty will have a way to contact me, I wonder if Lizzy should, too. Or maybe I should just let Lizzy and the children move on. She had become fond of all three of them and Lizzy was a super cook and baker. She hoped she knew someone who could help her out.*

Finally she drifted off to sleep thinking about the dinner tomorrow. Maybe she would ask Lizzy to make something for her to take.

WEDNESDAY DAWNED EARLY. Dani would have to take Misty to court to present her case for divorce to the judge. She had arranged it to have Misty's name legally changed to Michelle West as soon as the judge gave the approval for divorce. Once her name was changed they would file for a change of name on her credentials. She would be able to get her driver's license once she was established somewhere else.

Of course they would have to wait until the judge ruled on Lizzy's divorce before they could do anything about a name change or documents for her and the kids. Lizzy is not scheduled until next week along with Margo Hunter. She would have Maureen call Margo today and set up a time to sign her divorce papers.

Dani knew she was forgetting something as she went into the tunnel to make sure Misty was awake. She heard the shower running so turned back into the tunnel for a bit to give Misty privacy. She waited a good ten minutes and began whistling as she made her way to the chamber.

Misty was laughing, "You never could whistle a tune." She finished putting on her shoes and joined Dani heading into the main house.

She had made the bed and stored all her belongings before Dani had arrived. Knowing she was going to court she left off any make-up. The judge should see exactly what she endured at the hands of Rocky Evons.

They slipped out of the closet when Dani heard the children's voices downstairs. "Coast is clear."

Next stop was the dining room where breakfast was waiting for them. They ate with Lizzy and the kids. Dani excused herself to get all the papers ready they would need in court. She also asked Maureen to call Margo Hunter and get divorce papers typed up for her and for Lizzy. She picked up her file and put it in her briefcase, then went to find Lizzy.

"Lizzy, I need to ask a favor of you," Dani said entering the dining room.

"Anything, Miss Dani."

"I am going to a potluck dinner tonight," Dani explained. "I want to wow one of the people there with something you made. I am hoping to get backing for your new venture."

Lizzy smiled, "I won't disappoint you, Miss Dani. You just let me worry about it."

"Thank you."

"No," Lizzy shook her head, "it is me who should be thanking you."

Misty grabbed a jacket and the two women headed for the courthouse.

AFTER PASSING THROUGH the metal detectors at the front of the courthouse the two women went to the assigned courtroom and found seats. Dani sensed Misty's nervousness. She reached over and took her hand.

"It's going to be okay," Dani assured her. By the time it's posted in the newspaper you will be someone else living somewhere else."

Misty squeezed her hand, "I'm trusting you with my life."

"And I'm going to take good care of it."

They waited silently. There were not many people in the courtroom. The judge would come in and call off names to see who was there. He would proceed with cases where both parties were there. If the other party did not show up and Dani knew he would not, the judge would look at the case and decide whether or not to rule. One look at Misty would give the judge reason to rule.

The bailiff stood off to the side and said, "All rise for the Honorable Judge Andrew Welsh." Everyone rose as Judge Welsh entered and took his seat.

"Be seated," he said as a staffer put a stack of files on his right.

"I will be calling parties to each case before me today to see who is here. Those who have both parties present will be called first," the judge told them.

"Baker vs Baker," the judge said. "Is Mrs. Baker present?"

"No, your Honor," came a voice from the gallery.

"Is Mr. Baker present?"

"Yes, you Honor." A gentleman stood acknowledging the judge.

"We'll set you aside," the judge responded. "Simons vs Simons, are the parties here?"

A woman stood saying, "Yes, your Honor."

Immediately a man stood responding, "Yes, your Honor."

"Good you will be case number one," the judge said.

The judge read through several others finding one or two more cases in which both parties were present. "Evons vs Evons, are the parties here?"

Misty stood and replied, "Yes, your honor?" Then she sat.

The judge had looked up when Misty stood. He asked, "Is Mr. Evons present?"

Dani stood, "No, your Honor, he is incarcerated in the Rivers County jail awaiting sentencing."

"Thank you," the judge shuffled some papers, made a notation, and looked at Misty again. "You will be my last case today."

Misty nodded.

The judge asked one more time, "Has anyone entered the courtroom who has a case and has not been called?"

No one stood. Satisfied he had given everyone an opportunity he said, "Case one Simons vs Simons."

Both came forward and took seats. Mrs. Simons as the filer on the right and Mr. Simons as the defendant. They were sworn in by the bailiff and told to take seats. The judge read through the documents filed to refresh himself with the case.

Dani gave Misty's hand a squeeze. They would be sitting in the courtroom for a while.

The judge made short work of most of the cases. Ones with children took longer. Most of those were required to wait six months then return for a judgment. As always the courts tried to keep families together. Something which made Dani cringe when she thought of Lizzy and the kids. Finally the judge called, "Evons vs Evons will the parties step forward."

Dani and Misty walked toward the right side of the court room. "Be seated."

They sat and the bailiff swore them both in while the judge looked through the file.

"Mrs. Evons, do you have children?"

"No, your Honor."

"I see no reason why this divorce shouldn't be granted immediately." The judge's gavel came down.

The doors to the court room slammed open a moment later. Three burley men walked in. "What is the meaning of this?" Judge Welsh asked.

"We came to protest the divorce of our brother, Rocky Evons," one of the men said.

"There is nothing to protest," the judge told them. "The divorce has been granted. You gentlemen need to leave my courtroom at once."

"We ain't leaving without our sister-in-law," the same man responded.

Dani turned so she was shielding Misty. The bailiff had already called for reinforcements and they were coming through the doors.

"You are leaving or you will be held in contempt," Judge Welsh warned them. "This court has been adjourned."

The one who had spoken started walking toward Misty. Dani stood up holding her ground.

She was surprised when Misty spoke, "The judge just granted my divorce. I am no longer your sister-in-law. Go home before you find yourself in jail with Rocky. It's done."

He stopped in his tracks when Misty spoke, "It ain't over you stupid bitch. We will find you and bring you home." Then he turned as suddenly as he had entered and the three of them left.

Misty whispered to Dani, "They will be waiting outside for us."

"I have a plan," Dani assured her.

Once the courtroom had been cleared, the bailiff offered to see the women outside. "I can offer you an escort to your car."

"But you cannot stop them from following us," Misty said.

Dani reached for her hand and gave it a squeeze. "Do you have a phone I can use?"

"Right this way," the bailiff led them out a side door into a private room. "I'll wait outside."

Once inside Dani picked up the phone and dialed Brad's number.

"Stevens' Construction," Maxie answered.

"Maxie, it's Dani. I have an emergency is Brad in?"

"One moment." Then she was on hold.

"Dani, are you okay?" came Brad's concerned voice.

"For the moment," she answered. "I need you to pick up Misty at the rear of the courthouse and take her up river to my dock. Can you do it?"

"I'll be there in five minutes," was the reply then the phone was disconnected.

Turning to Misty she said, "I have it covered."

"What did you mean up river?" Misty asked.

"Please, don't ask questions," Dani said. "Do everything Brad tells you and you will be safe in the house without anyone knowing."

Misty was confused, but nodded in agreement.

Dani walked to the door and said to the bailiff, "I have someone coming to pick Misty up at the back door of the courthouse. After they are gone, you may escort me to my car."

"I need to let the underground guard know someone is coming. What will he be driving?" the bailiff asked.

"Probably his blue pick-up truck," Dani replied.

The bailiff radioed the information to the underground guard and led the women toward the area. Brad was waiting when they arrived.

He hugged Dani, "Are you sure you're okay?"

"I'm fine. Misty will need to keep her head down until you get to the boat," she told him.

Brad turned to Misty, "Let's put you on the back seat where you can lay down." He helped her into the truck then tossed a blanket over her. "We won't be in the truck long."

Misty's muffled, "I'm good," was all he needed to hear. He hugged Dani and got into the truck to drive away.

The bailiff and Dani returned to the courthouse and he walked her out the front door to her car. "Good luck to you, Miss," he said as she got into her car.

"Thank you for your help." Then she was driving out of the parking lot. She watched her rearview mirror for signs she was being followed. Making a few unneeded turns to be sure no one was on her tail. Satisfied, she called Brad on his cell phone. She got his voice mail and left him a message, "No, tail so I am heading home. I love you." She continued to be vigilant all the way home. When she suspected her vehicle was being tailed she made a turn. Letting out a breath every time the car did not turn. She saw no cars or trucks which looked the same, so she felt safe.

Arriving at home she parked her car in the garage and entered the house through the kitchen. Ella looked up surprised to see her alone.

"It's okay, Brad is bringing her by water," Dani answered the unasked question. "Rocky's brothers showed up after the judge had granted the divorce."

Without another word, Dani left the kitchen and made her way upstairs. She stepped into the closet closing the door behind her and ran down to the chamber. She kept running on through the tunnel until she got to the door, unlocking it, she raced to the dock. Listening carefully she heard the sound of an outboard. She hoped it was Brad with Misty.

Less than five minutes later Dani let out the breath she had been holding. Brad rounded the curve with Misty in the front of his boat. They appeared to be safe. They pulled into the dock and Misty threw Dani the rope to tie off the front of the boat. Brad cut the engine and tied off the back. He stepped out of the boat onto the dock and then turned to give Misty a hand.

"Where on earth are we?" Misty asked looking around.

"This is the back of my property," Dani said smiling. "Follow me." She turned leading the way to the tunnel into the chamber. Brad locked the door behind him.

"Wow," was all Misty could say. "I had no idea how safe I'd be here."

"I told Ella you were coming this way, she was relieved," Dani said. "Now I have to get ready for dinner tonight."

"Come out this way with me," Brad suggested.

"Misty, lock this door behind us and open it for no one," Dani told her.

The three trooped back down the tunnel. Brad and Dani stepped outside and listened for the sound of the deadbolt. Then they walked to the dock. As Dani untied the front of the boat and Brad untied the back he said, "I'll be back in about forty-five minutes to get you for the cook-out."

She tossed the rope into the boat, blew him a kiss, and scampered toward the backyard. Brad headed back for town thinking, *she will be the death of me. I never want her to be in danger. What have I signed on for? Smiling like this was an everyday adventure. Geez.*

FORTY-FIVE MINUTES LATER, Dani was seated in Brad's truck a bowl of grape salad between them and a plate of Lizzy's baked goods on top of the bowl. Dani had her briefcase between her legs.

"So is this a working dinner?" Brad asked.

"Nope, I'm saving all the work for later. I just want us to meet Macy's friends."

"Okay." *Somehow he suspected it would turn to work. He'd better get used to it, if he planned to marry the feisty woman beside him.*

They arrived to find a Jeep, another truck, and a car in the driveway. "This is going to be a bigger shindig than I thought," Brad said.

"Do you want to leave?"

"Nope, I want to mix and mingle," he answered. "Eli will be here won't he?"

Just then Eli came out the front door. He waved when he saw them. "Glad you could make it."

He took the food from Dani and led the way inside. Macy was in the kitchen. "Look who I found in the driveway."

Macy turned around, let out a squeal, and was hugging Dani before she could say a word. Then she turned to shake hands with Brad. "JJ and Sally Mae are outside. You'll be able to spot them, Sally Mae is showing off her new engagement ring. My partner, Tom and his wife Shannon are here too. They belong to the boys you will see running around in the yard. Make yourself at home, there are drinks in the cooler."

Brad, his hand in the small of Dani's back, followed Eli out to the deck. Brad was impressed with the deck and hot tub. The yard was well tended. The two boys Macy mentioned were shooting hoops at a moveable basket.

Eli quickly introduced them, "This is JJ and his soon to be wife, Sally Mae, and this stunning couple is Tom and Shannon Maxwell. The gorgeous little doll in the walker there is Mimi. I'd like you all to meet Brad Stevens and Dani Montgomery."

Brad and Dani found themselves surrounded by people giving them a hearty welcome. They found the cooler with drinks and before they knew it dinner was served. Toasts were made to JJ and Sally Mae. The steaks were perfect and Dani got raves on the salad and desserts.

As the sun lowered in the sky, Tom and Shannon announced they were heading home. JJ and Sally Mae were soon to follow as they wanted to share their news with Ida before it got too late.

Dani started picking up the last of the items on the table. Macy came back to help her. "Can we talk?" Dani asked.

"Sure, leave those. I'll get Eli to clean up."

"I'd like to talk to both of you, but we should probably do it inside."

"Well, let's get this done then," Macy chuckled. *She hoped Dani had found something in Chelsie Patton's medical records.*

Inside, Eli had the dishwasher almost filled. He took the things from Macy and Dani saying, "I'll bring coffee into the living room in a minute."

Brad stayed to help Eli with clean up. They made coffee and tea, put it with cream and sugar on Macy's serving tray, then headed in to join the ladies.

As everybody settled in, Dani began, "I have several things I'd like to discuss and I want to start with the most pleasant."

"Go for it, Dani, we're listening," Macy replied, then took a sip of her tea.

"Eli, I need you honest opinion as a chef about the salad and baked goods I brought tonight."

"Wow, I didn't know I was supposed to be giving a critique," he chuckled. "I have made it before, but I added brown sugar to the walnuts. I liked it better without the brown sugar. As to the baked goods, I'm not a pastry chef, but those are some of the best I've ever eaten."

"They were made by one of my battered women," Dani told them. "Her dream is to open a bakery and restaurant in a small town. She makes her grandmother's recipes from memory. I can get her on the path out of town with a new identity, but I don't have the funding for opening a bakery or restaurant."

Brad chimed in, "Eli, what if you and I go scouting small towns and see if we can get a building cheap? I'll provide the labor and materials to bring it up to code and make it look wonderful."

"It's a great idea," Eli replied. "I can put up enough money to give her supplies for the first six months."

"Can it be a building she could also live in?" Dani interjected.

"If we can find one with a park nearby so the kids will have a place to play," Brad insisted.

"You guys are the best," Dani informed them.

"So, now we have that all taken care of, what's the bad news?" Macy asked.

Dani reached for her briefcase. Brad rolled his eyes, and poured another cup of coffee.

"I have gone over the medical files sent to me regarding Chelsie Patton," Dani began. "Something happened to this girl before she ever went to the camp. I'd really like to see photos of her from age one to age eleven. I want to know when the change took place." She passed the photo of Chelsie taken when she was admitted and the one when she was about to be released. "Look at her eyes. They were empty when she arrived and they were empty, yet somehow determined when she left."

"Holy cow!" Macy exclaimed. "I would never have pictured her as a fat child. I see what you're saying about her eyes."

"Some kind of abuse," Eli said. "Must have been someone she trusted, father, uncle, other family member, or friend."

Brad shook his head, "What makes you say that?"

"Her eyes in the first photo," Eli explained. "She has shut off her emotions. She has pulled within herself. How does she act around others?"

Macy rolled her eyes, "The girl thinks she is superior to everyone. She is often rude and belligerent."

"I maintain my assessment, she's been abused," Eli stated. "It's a good idea to look at earlier photos. Nice catch, Dani."

"Thanks. I'd also like to know if she still keeps a journal or does yoga."

"Why?" Macy asked.

"She started both while in the clinic," Dani told them. "The excerpts from them are cold and do not really allow her feelings to surface. The yoga is something she writes about as if it gives her power. She also meditated near a brook or stream on the property. I wondered if she retained any of these when she was released."

"We can ask," Macy said. "I don't know what her condition is since she collapsed in the court room."

"Maybe when I come to Rivers Edge on Friday, we should meet with Sarah Stephens."

"I'll arrange it. What time do you have to be in court?"

Dani pulled out her appointment book, "I have to be there for sentencing at ten in the morning. After we are done, I have to serve Rocky Evons with his divorce papers."

Macy was making notes, "Let's see if we can get Sarah to join us for lunch and I'll bring Tom with me."

"It works for me."

The two couples collected the coffee cups, Dani returned things to her briefcase while the men took things back to the kitchen.

Macy chuckled when she heard Eli say, "Man's duty is always clean up."

Brad just laughed.

Hugging Macy, Dani said, "This was wonderful. I'd love to do this again."

"We will, believe me, we will," Macy assured her.

Eli and Macy walked out with Brad and Dani, the women hugged again as the men shook hands. "She's a special woman you have, Brad."

"I agree."

As they got in the car and backed out the driveway, Macy and Eli stood arm-in-arm, waving good-bye.

CHAPTER THIRTY-FIVE

s Macy and Eli entered the house, he asked, "Are you sure Dani wasn't a detective at one time?"

"No, she's always been an attorney," Macy told him. "She began working in the prosecutor's office. So, she knows what to look for."

"She's got a good perspective on your case," he continued. "I'd want her on my team. I hope Sarah Stephens appreciates her. I know Brad does. What do you think of her idea for the bakery restaurant?"

"I love it if you and Brad can pull it off, but it needs to be far enough away from here her abusive husband can't find her."

"Agreed, I'll give Brad a call in the morning to see where he thinks we should start looking."

"You like him, don't you?" Macy asked smiling.

"As a matter of fact, I do. I think he and Dani are good for each other and I'm glad you asked them to come tonight." Eli pulled Macy into his arms and kissed her. *He knew the minute he did, it was a mistake. He wanted so much more.* Breaking away from her, he said, "Much as I love you, I need to get home."

Macy leaned into him and whispered, "Stay."

"Not yet," he told her gently. "We have much to talk about before I stay. This is not the time." He gave her a kiss he hoped would convey this was not a rejection. Then he said, "Sleep well." Let himself out the door and left.

While Macy was disappointed, she knew he was right. They had much to talk about before they made the next leap. She locked the door and went up to bed.

BRAD HAD DANI tucked under his arm as he drove toward her house. "Did you think about sharing the restaurant idea with me before springing it tonight?"

She snuggled in closer, "We really haven't had much time for talking."

"Which brings me to another thing," Brad told her. "Are you always going to be in danger like you were today?"

"No, in fact, I wasn't in danger," she replied. "None of my other clients has crazed ex-brother-in-laws."

"I can't tell you how glad I was to see you on the dock," Brad said. "I was truly frightened."

"I'm sorry. I never intended for you to be worried about me."

"Dani, what part of I love you did you miss?"

She shoved her hand inside his shirt, "I didn't miss any of it."

He could feel her smiling against his chest and he felt earlier tension leaving him.

"I will support you in this, but I think we need a plan. What will happen if I am at a work site?"

"I'll think of something."

"Which scares me even more," Brad confessed. "We need a plan."

"Okay, I'll work on a plan," Dani pouted. Changing the subject she asked, "Did you enjoy tonight?"

"I did. I like Macy and Eli and their friends. Besides I have to admit I was surprised at your insight into a case you barely know about."

"My first job was in the prosecutor's office, I have an idea what to look for in the 'bad guys'," she joked.

He chuckled saying, "I guess you would. Sure am glad you're on my team." Then he hugged her to him.

She hugged him back and snuggled into him. "Are you mad because I didn't tell you about the restaurant idea?"

"No, I was a bit shocked you had gone to so much trouble for Lizzy and the kids. It's the right thing to do."

Smiling she hugged him tighter, "I'll try to keep you more in the loop."

"I'll call Eli in the morning."

"Mmm hmm."

Brad looked down to see her nodding off to sleep. She was so beautiful. He almost hit the deer crossing in front of him, better keep his eyes on the road. As they turned into Dani's driveway, Brad found himself more reluctant than ever to let her go. Soon he knew he was going to propose.

He parked the truck, turned off the motor and looked at Dani sleeping in his arms. He eased himself out of the truck so he could carry her to the door. She felt light as he lifted her into his arms. He walked up the steps wondering where she kept her key, then he just tried the door. It had been left unlocked. He carried her in, closed the door, and went up to the stairs to her room. Dani's eyes fluttered open when he laid her on the bed.

"Are you planning to stay?"

"Not this time, Sweetheart," he whispered as he leaned in to kiss her.

She clung to him. Not only was he warm, he was filling her with passion. When he broke away he said, "Get ready for bed, I'll bring the dishes out of the truck and come say goodnight." He rose and quietly shut the door.

Dani quickly changed into her nightgown and slid into her bed. In spite of herself, she was asleep when her head hit the pillow.

Brad got the dishes from the truck, took them to the kitchen, rinsed them, and put them in the dishwasher. Then he headed up to say goodnight to Dani. He smiled seeing her already asleep. It had been quite a day for her. He walked to the bed, leaned down, and gave her a gentle kiss. Then he turned off the light by her bed and closed the door on his way out. As he left the house he made sure the front door was locked.

Slowly he drove home, going over in his mind how and when he would propose.

DANI STRETCHED WHEN she woke the next morning. She could not put a finger on her contentment, but she savored it. Then she slipped out of bed and down the hall to shower and get ready for the day. She had a meeting with Margo Hunter to get ready for her divorce proceedings on Friday morning. *She hoped it would be less stressful than Misty's had been. She would be sure to check and see if Margo had any crazed brother-in-laws beforehand.*

She just followed her nose to the dining room. Her hope had been to give Lizzy the good news this morning. The woman could sure use some. She heard the patter of small feet before she reached the bottom of the stairs. Chuckling she was surprised to see Teddy ready to pull out her chair.

"Why thank you kind, sir," she said smiling.

"Mom is bringing you a surprise breakfast," Amy told her.

"Well, she didn't have to do anything special," Dani assured them.

Teddy held Amy's chair and then climbed into his own. It did not take long for Ella to open the door from the kitchen. She was carrying a large pot of something smelling delicious. Lizzy followed with another tray on her lap. Ella set the pot in the center of the table and turned to take the tray from Lizzy so she could slide into her chair.

"Good morning," Lizzy said. "Teddy, will say grace?"

Teddy bowed his head and began, "Dear God, thank you for letting Miss Dani find us and help. Thank you for the food we are going to share. Amen."

There was a chorus of 'amens' from the ladies around the table.

Ella opened the pot and began serving everyone then she left them to eat. Lizzy passed the tray of biscuits around.

Once they all had food, Dani said, "I have a small announcement to make."

Teddy, Amy, and Lizzy all looked at her. Almost afraid of what she might say.

Dani seeing their frightened expressions quickly said, "It's good news."

Everyone let out a sigh of relief and began eating.

"I talked to some friends of mine last night. They are going out today to see about finding a building in a small town to remodel into a restaurant and bakery. Lizzy, you will be able to pick out the decorations, but they will need a name so be thinking of one. I also know you will be getting six months of supplies and enough money to pay for help for the first six months."

Lizzy dropped her spoon. She was too stunned to say anything. This woman who came into her life, rescued her and her children from unimagined horrors, was now telling her a lifelong dream was going to come true. She cried tears of joy.

"Mom, are you okay?" Teddy asked anxiously.

"Mommy, don't cry," Amy said reaching for her mother's hand.

"It's okay, kids, I think those are happy tears," Dani told them.

Lizzy wiped her eyes, nodding in the affirmative. The children settled back to their breakfast. Lizzy had made oatmeal with apples, raisins, and cinnamon. The butter biscuits were the best Dani had ever eaten.

As she finished her breakfast, Dani was thinking of all she had to do today. First was Margo Hunter, this afternoon was Lizzy. She also needed to check on Misty. She excused herself and headed to the office.

Maureen was already at her desk with a cup of coffee. "Good morning, Miss Dani."

"Wonderful morning, Maureen," Dani replied. "Margo Hunter will be in this morning and we will go over her papers for her divorce on Friday. I don't want any surprises like yesterday. Also Lizzy's dream of a restaurant and bakery could very well come true."

Maureen looked at her boss in awe, "I'm so glad I work for you."

"Thank you. Just doing my job."

"And doing it remarkably well," Maureen told her.

Dani smiled, "I have a couple of calls to make before Mrs. Hunter arrives." She walked into her office, closed the door, poured herself a cup of coffee, and settled down to call a couple of her contacts in what she called the underground movement.

CHAPTER THIRTY-SIX

At ten o'clock, Maureen knocked on Dani's door, opened it, and led Margo Hunter into the room. Maureen handed Dani a folder, and asked, "Would either of you ladies like some coffee?"

"Please, thank you," Margo replied.

Dani just nodded yes.

Maureen filled their cups and left the room closing the door.

"I have a couple questions before we get into your divorce papers," Dani began. "Do you have any in-laws who might show up in court to protest you getting a divorce?"

"No, what makes you ask?"

"I had a case yesterday where after the judge made his decision, the in-laws came in and threatened the person getting the divorce."

Margo laughed, "I'm an orphan and Evan is an only child."

Good, let's go over your divorce papers. We'll be on the early docket in Rivers Edge tomorrow morning."

When they were done, Dani asked Maureen to come witness the signature. Maureen came in followed by Ella. They signed as witnesses after Margo. Then Dani put them in a file for morning.

"Margo, I have an afternoon case and a meeting with the ADA in Rivers Edge are you going to be able to get to the courthouse?" Dani asked.

"I'll be there at nine sharp."

"Very well, I'll meet you there," Dani assured her.

Margo left and Maureen went to see if she could find Lizzy. Those were the next divorce papers to go over.

LIZZY CAME IN and Maureen got her some coffee. She shut the door leaving Lizzy and Dani to go over the divorce papers.

"Miss Dani," Lizzy began tentatively, "I don't know how you managed to get people interested in my dream. I only know I will never be able to repay you."

"Lizzy, I have never asked for payment. I am just doing my job."

"No," Lizzy shook her head, "Your job was to get me to file for divorce. You took my children in when there was no one else. You have given me a home and hope. It wasn't just your job. You have a beautiful heart."

Dani blushed, "Thank you, Lizzy. In part I am repaying a debt to a friend."

"I don't know who your friend is," Lizzy told her, "But I think they will consider the debt paid."

Nodding, Dani continued, "We need to go over your divorce papers, including sole custody of the children."

Lizzy picking up on the change of subject said, "Okay."

The women spent the next hour going over the papers making sure Lizzy understood everything in them. Then Dani asked Maureen and Ella to come in and witness Lizzy's signature. When they were done the two women left, as Lizzy was turning to leave she asked Dani, "Miss Dani, will I be able to change my name?"

"Of course, Lizzy, do you have an idea what you want it to be?"

"Yes, I want to be Beth Argyle, it was my grandmother's maiden name."

"Do you want the children's names changed?" Dani asked.

"Just their last names. I want them to be Argyles, too."

"I'll see it is done."

Lizzy rolled her chair out saying, "Thank you."

Dani watched her go, knowing she should have said more. Talking about Michelle was not easy and telling strangers was not something she felt obligated to do. *She had opened her home to Lizzy and the children, but she did not have to open her private life, or did she? Did she need to explain how she became involved with battered women?* She shook her head to clear her thoughts. She needed to check on Misty.

MAKING SURE NO one would see her, Dani slipped into the linen closet and down the tunnel. As she got closer she called out to Misty letting her know she was coming.

"Come on down, Dani," Misty yelled.

Dani entered the chamber to see Misty had everything together and was curled up with a book, music played softly in the background.

"You look like you're adjusting to this," Dani observed.

Misty shut her book, "It could be worse. I get lonely, but keep telling myself it is just temporary."

"It is," Dani assured her. "I'm really sorry for the way things turned out. I have made some calls and we are hoping to move you tomorrow night. The next stop on your journey you'll get your new identification. I wish I could have done it for you."

"You did plenty," Misty said. "I'd have been dragged back to live with Rocky's brothers as a slave until Rocky gets out. Then the beatings would start again. This is a castle compared to what my life would have been."

"Well, it isn't the last stop on your road to freedom."

"Nope, and if it weren't for you, I wouldn't have this chance." Misty stood and spun in a circle with her arms out. "I'll never forget this place and how it helped me. God willing I will have a chance to help someone, else." She pulled Dani into her arms. "Thank you, old friend."

Dani hugged Misty back, her mind going to the years they had spent growing up. This was almost good bye and Dani did not know if she was ready for it. She sniffed and broke the hug.

"I know you'll be fine."

"Yeah, Aunt Ella is sure I will be, too. It seems anything you touch is golden as far as she's concerned. So, I'm going to make sure it rubs off on me. As she says, not many people get a second chance," Misty ended her mini speech.

"Just don't start grumbling under your breath," Dani said chuckling.

Misty laughed at the reference. "Naw, I'm okay."

"I want to go out the river exit, will you follow me and lock the door behind me?"

"Sure thing, just let me know when I need to be ready tomorrow."

The two made their way down the tunnel to the door Brad had installed. Dani turned to hug Misty once more. "I love you, Misty."

"Yeah, me, too." Misty let Dani go and slid the deadbolt on the door. It was a lonely walk back to the chamber room.

CHAPTER THIRTY-SEVEN

Walking the perimeter of her lawn, Dani breathed deeply of the early autumn air. *She loved the Willows, it was her home, safe haven, port in a storm. Was she putting it all at risk? Should she risk her sanctuary to create one for others? The goal had been to bring justice to those who could escape unlike Michelle, whom she could not protect. Was putting a future with Brad in jeopardy? Would he want to raise children knowing others slept in the secret room? Maybe she should talk to Brad about it, he might have a different perspective. He might hate the idea of what she was doing altogether. Had she used his feelings for her to coerce him into something he didn't believe in? Was she simply being selfish?* All these thoughts ran through her head as she made her way to the back door. She paused listening as Teddy and Amy laughed with their mother about something on the TV. *Nope, she was doing the right thing.*

She entered quietly so as not to disturb the young family and made her way to her office. Maureen looked up.

"No, calls, Miss Dani," she said.

"Thanks, Maureen, go ahead and go home," Dani told her. "I'll be in Rivers Edge most of the day tomorrow."

"If you're sure you won't need me," Maureen hesitated. "Is everything all right?"

Dani chuckled, "Just second guessing myself, nothing to worry about."

Maureen started to put things in order, "I'm glad to be a part of what you are doing. I only wish I could contribute more."

Looking at Maureen, Dani decided she was serious. "I'll see if we can expand your aide. We'll keep it on the down low for you though."

Smiling Maureen finished and got her things to leave. "Thank you, Miss Dani."

Dani nodded, she had Margo's divorce tomorrow, the conference with Macy, Tom, and Sarah Stephens, and the conviction of Rocky Evons. Then the escorting of Misty to her next destination. Margo would be gone the following day and soon, Lizzy and the kids would be gone. She sighed and sat at her desk.

THE NEXT TIME Dani looked up it was to see Brad standing in the doorway. She smiled as she stood up and walked to where he was standing. "I've been thinking about you, today," she told him walking into his arms.

"Good thoughts I hope."

"Mmm hmm," she moaned as he enclosed her in his arms and kissed her.

Dani lost herself in the feeling of being in Brad's arms until she felt a tug on her arm. She pulled apart and looked down. Amy was wide-eyed and staring up at her.

"Hi, Amy," Dani hoped she didn't sound as breathless as she felt.

"I'm 'posed to tell you dinner is ready," Amy said.

"Well, I for one am glad you did," Brad said sweeping the little girl into his arms.

She giggled and Dani collected herself as they made their way to the dining room.

"What's so funny?" Teddy asked as they entered.

"Mr. Brad was kissing Miss Dani," Amy announced.

Dani blushed as she took her seat. Brad put Amy in her seat and sat down.

"That's disgusting, Amy," Teddy told her.

"Why?"

"It just is."

"Teddy, some day you will feel differently," Brad assured him.

"I doubt it."

They stopped talking as Ella and Lizzy entered carrying the night's dinner. Ella made sure everyone was served before she left. Lizzy had again outdone herself.

"Do you mind, Miss Dani, if I get Maureen to type some of my recipes?" Lizzy asked.

"Not at all," Dani replied. "In fact, I told her to do so if you asked."

"Good, I want to share them with Ella. She has been so kind about letting me take over her kitchen. She is also going to share some of her recipes with me," explained Lizzy.

Dani nodded in agreement, "It will also be a good legacy to leave your children."

"Someday I might make them into a cookbook to sell in my business," Lizzy dreamed.

Brad chimed in as if on cue, "I scouted some places today. We haven't found the perfect place yet, but we'll be looking again tomorrow."

Lizzy smiled. Dinner was pretty much silent until Teddy and Amy asked to be excused.

Dani looked at Lizzy and said, "Go, join your children. Brad and I can handle clean-up."

Smiling Lizzy wheeled away to follow her two children.

BRAD HELPED DANI carry dishes into the kitchen. She rinsed, put them in the dishwasher, and started it. Then she turned to make coffee. Brad carried the tray of coffee to Dani's office.

Once there they both sat and Brad said, "So, what were you thinking about me today?"

"Actually I was thinking of asking your advice," she began then took a sip of her coffee. "I was having doubts about what I am doing."

"You mean, helping Misty, Lizzy and her kids?"

Dani nodded, "I was wondering if I was putting my own future at risk. If I was asking too much of others for a cause which truly belongs only to me. Then I heard Lizzy and the kids laughing."

"If I was dead set against it, do you think I'd have dropped everything to come rescue you and Misty?" questioned Brad.

She set her cup on the desk and turned to look at him, "I was questioning whether or not I had used your feelings for me to coerce you into this."

"My feelings aside, I think this is a wonderful thing you are doing," he told her. "If you had not convinced Lizzy to press charges, I doubt we'd ever see her alive again."

She took Brad's cup, set it on her desk, and leaned into him. "I love you. I have always loved you, and I always will." Then she kissed him taking his breath away.

When she broke the kiss he pulled her back saying, "My turn," as he kissed her again.

A tentative knock at the door brought them both back to reality. Teddy and Amy stood there staring.

"Hi, guys," Dani said. "Ready to be tucked into bed?"

Teddy looked at both of them strangely then answered, "Yeah, we are."

"I told him where to look for you," Amy piped in.

"Good thing you did," Brad told her. "How about I take you up and Miss Dani can look in on you when she comes up?"

"Sounds okay," Teddy said turning and heading out of the office.

Brad lifted Amy up while Dani took their cups and the tray to the kitchen. She rinsed the cups and left them in the sink. *Teddy is not happy with Brad and me. Wish I knew why he disapproves all the sudden? Guess it's time to find out.* She shut off the lights on her way out.

She waited as Brad came smiling down the stairs. "I promised I'd send you right up."

"Of course you did," she smirked.

"Dani, I love you, too," he said kissing her gently. "We need to do some talking when some of this settles down."

"I'm all for it," she assured him.

"Lock the door before you go up." Brad slipped out and she locked the door.

It was time to go face the music. Softly she walked up the stairs to say goodnight to the kids.

WALKING INTO THE children's room Dani pasted a smile on her face. "Hey, guys, time to call it a day."

"Why, Miss Dani?" Teddy asked as she began tucking Amy in.

She looked at Teddy, "Why what?"

Teddy crossed his arms trying to look indignant, "Would you kiss Mr. Brad?"

"Oh, when people love each other they kiss," she told him.

"But you know what happens," Teddy insisted.

"Hopefully, we will get married and have children," Dani whispered.

Teddy gave her a look of incredulity, "Miss Dani, men pretend to love women, give them children, and then beat them senseless when they are not perfect."

"Oh, Teddy," she walked to his bed and sat down. "Not all men are like your dad. Some men continue to love their wives and children. I wanted to give your mom a chance to get away and give you and Amy a better life." Dani took his hand. "I want your mom to find someone who will appreciate how wonderful she is and want to be a real dad to you and Amy."

"Are you sure?"

"I'm very sure," she kissed him on the forehead as she tucked him in. "I want you all to be happy and to have a real family. It's going to take a long time before your mom trusts another man, but when she does, promise me you will give him a chance."

Teddy nodded, "I will."

"Me, too," Amy added not wanting to be left out.

"Now do you think you can sleep?" Dani asked.

"Yes," they answered in unison.

She smiled and let herself out of the room. She walked to her bedroom wondering how much damage their dad had done to them with his actions. She pulled on pj's and climbed into bed. *If Teddy thinks kissing is bad because it leads to beatings, what else does he think men should do? Lord, please help these children to heal. Amen.* She turned on her side and fell asleep.

CHAPTER THIRTY-EIGHT

Up before the sun, Dani showered and dressed for the day. She checked on the children then went directly to the kitchen. Ella was just putting the coffee on.

"Is something wrong?" Ella asked.

"No, but Misty will be leaving tonight. I thought you might want to spend a little time with her."

"I'll go right now," Ella said. She picked up a small basket as she went.

Dani looked around for something simple to eat. She came across some of Lizzy's cinnamon rolls, by the time the coffee was ready, the cinnamon roll was coming out of the microwave. Dani poured a cup of coffee and went to her office.

She double checked all the files she needed for the day, finished her breakfast, and left a note for Maureen giving her schedule and to let her know she would check in the first break she had. With her briefcase in hand, Dani shut the door to her office and headed to her car. She put everything on the passenger seat, got in, and started off to Rivers Edge.

Halfway to Rivers Edge her cell phone rang, "Hello."

"I thought since you had a long day today, I'd pick you up and take you to the cabin for dinner," Brad's voice sounded husky. Dani's pulse quickened.

"What a wonderful idea."

"Good, I'll call Ella and let her know she will be short two for dinner. See you later."

"Later," she echoed as she hung up. *She might salvage something out of the day after all. Darn, she forgot Brad would have to take Misty back downriver tonight so she could connect with her ride to a new life. She'd call him later on her break.*

Dani arrived at the courthouse before nine o'clock, parked, and went through security. She checked on which courtroom the case would be heard in, then made a call to Margo to see where she was.

"I should be pulling in any minute now," Margo told her.

"Look for me in the hallway."

Dani waited near the security desk.

In less than a minute, Margo made her way through the security check. The two women went into the courtroom and found seats near the front. Dani was not sure where they were on the docket. They waited but only four others joined them in the gallery.

The bailiff entered and said, "All rise for the Honorable Adele Latham." Everyone rose as Judge Latham entered. She was a tall woman with salt and pepper hair. Dani was unsure what to expect.

"Please be seated," Judge Latham said. "Bailiff, call the first case."

"Hunter vs Hunter for the purpose of divorce."

Dani and Margo rose and approached the plaintiff table. Dani saying, "Danielle Montgomery for the plaintiff."

"And the defendant?"

"Is currently in the county lock-up in Windham County on a charge of battery and will be there for the next fifteen years," Dani replied.

The judge took a good look at Margo, "Mrs. Hunter, please step forward."

Margo stepped toward the judge's bench. "These bruises I see, are they a result of a beating by your husband?"

"Yes, your Honor."

"You may step back."

Margo returned to stand next to Dani.

"This court grants the divorce in favor of Mrs. Hunter. Are there any properties to be divided?"

"Mrs. Hunter wants nothing from this union but her freedom, your Honor," Dani answered.

"With nothing left to discuss, I grant the divorce. You may pick up your papers on your way out." Her gavel banged. Dani and Margo left as the bailiff was getting the next case ready.

"How can my papers be ready so quick?" Margo asked when they were in the hall.

"The court reporter now types everything into a computer. When the decree is given she hits send and papers can be picked up in the clerk's office," Dani told her. "We no longer have to wait for a transcript to be typed."

"Great, what happens to me now?"

"Go to wherever you are staying pack everything. Meet me in the parking lot here at three and I'll lead you to someone who will give you a new identity and get you started on the rest of your trip."

Margo hugged Dani, who was caught completely off guard. "I can't thank you enough for saving my life."

"You are very welcome," Dani replied. "You will do fine."

They picked up Margo's divorce papers and she waved a cheery good-bye to Dani as she went to pack her meager things."

WHEN MARGO LEFT Dani called Macy. She put her briefcase in her car and stood next to it making her call.

"McVannel."

"Macy, it's Dani."

"Sarah told me to tell you she's in courtroom four on the second floor. Go in and sit where she can see you. She had your guy brought up in case you got done early."

"Super," Dani said. "I just finished. I'll call you for lunch."

"Sounds good."

The two hung up, Dani reached for her briefcase, locked her car, and headed back into the courthouse. She went through security again and asked where courtroom four was. Following the directions she was given, she slipped into the back of the courtroom. As soon as the judge's gavel came down, she made her way toward the front of the room.

Sarah turned as if she sensed Dani. They locked eyes, and Dani took a seat. Sarah motioned to the bailiff. She spoke to him in soft tones. He nodded and went out through a side door. When he re-entered he nodded to Sarah and called the next case.

Dani sat through three cases one was a plea agreement, another asked for an extension. This one was being heard before the judge. When it was over, the bailiff called the next case.

"Rivers County vs Rocky Evons"

Rocky was led in and Dani took her place beside him at the defendants table.

"I see this is a plea agreement."

Sarah spoke, "Yes, your, Honor."

He looked at Dani, "Both parties have agreed?"

"Yes, your, Honor."

"Rocky Evons have you agreed to this plea agreement?"

"Yes, your, Honor."

"In that case, your sentence will be fifteen to twenty years and you will serve the full fifteen before you are eligible for parole." As he said it the judge brought his gavel down. "You may take the prisoner away."

Rocky was still in shock as he was led away. At least he was not as threatening as his brothers had been. Dani picked up her briefcase nodded to Sarah and went to call Macy about lunch.

THE TWO FRIENDS met at Dollie's Deli. They took a table at the back. Both ordering chicken salad sandwiches and iced tea. When the waitress left, Macy began, "So, how's your project going?"

"I have two going out today. One this afternoon and one tonight."

"Are you sure you want to keep this up?"

Dani thought for a minute, "Yes, I heard Lizzy and the kids laughing together the other day and I knew I was doing the right thing."

Macy sighed, "Sometimes I wish I had the gumption to do something like this."

"You are," Dani assured her, "every time you refer someone to me."

"I suppose."

The waitress arrived with their orders and the two began to eat. Conversation ceased for a few minutes.

Dani asked, "Is Tom going to be at the meeting with Sarah?"

"He wouldn't miss it. By the way, Eli thinks you'd make a great detective if you ever want to change professions."

Chuckling Dani almost choked on her tea. "He can't be serious."

"Think about all the stuff you managed to learn just by reading her medical file," Macy countered. "You were the one who saw something in her eyes none of us picked up on."

"You would have."

"I like to think so, but I'm not sure," Macy confessed. "I think we were so wrapped up in how evil she was, we couldn't see there was something else going on."

"We'll have to see if she ever comes up for trial again. I'd like to be there."

They finished their lunch, walked to the police station to pick up Tom, and the three of them walked to Sarah's office in the courthouse.

The secretary showed them right into a conference room. Sarah joined them a few minutes later.

"Thank you all for coming," Sarah started. "I understand Miss Montgomery has found something in Chelsie Patton's medical files which could have bearing on our case."

Dani gave everyone the file she had prepared. "I asked to have a cork board brought in as I know Macy likes to see the lines connect."

Macy smiled.

"The first photo you see in the file is Chelsie Patton at age twelve," Dani put the photo on the board. "Look closely at her eyes. See the vacant look?"

"What is the significance," Sarah asked.

Tom spoke in answer, "We see this kind of vacant look in sociopaths."

Sarah looked again at the photo. "I see she was much heavier at twelve than she is now."

"There might be a reason," Macy injected.

"Please look at the next photo of Chelsie. It was taken the day she was released," Dani said as she hung the photo on the board next to the first one.

Sarah was first to comment, "Her eyes look harsher. Almost as if she has reached a decision."

"Wow!" Tom said, "She's gone from blank, vacant sociopath eyes to evil determination."

"I asked Macy to see if she could get photos of a younger Chelsie," Dani told them. She sent me this packet earlier this week. In your folders you will find copies. The next one you see is a happy one year old Chelsie." She put the photo on the board while the others looked at it.

Sarah was a bit indignant, "She's a baby for heavens, sake. What are we going to see from this?"

"Bear with me," Dani asked, "I want to show you when you first find a change in Chelsie's eyes. It will tell us something we need to know."

"I get it," Tom's expression showed he did. "You want to show us a progression of photos hoping to find when this happy baby changed to what we see at twelve."

Nodding Dani posted the next photo, "The next one shows you Chelsie at age two, still a smiling happy toddler."

Everyone agreed so Dani posted the photo of three year old Chelsie followed by a photo when she was four.

Macy was quick to point out, "Her early childhood seems to have been happy. Photos after this will be school photos."

Dani posted Chelsie's kindergarten photo. When there was no discussion she posted the first grade photo and the second grade photo. Still no one made a comment.

They turned to the third grade photo and Sarah made an audible gasp. "How old was she in in this photo?"

"Eight going on nine," Dani answered.

"Something has changed in her life," Tom said. "It's not the vacant stare, but something is different."

"I agree," Sarah said. "I want to see more."

The fourth grade photo went up and they all looked at it. "It seems to have gotten worse," Macy said. "Look at how much weight she's gained."

"Eating disorder in one so young?" Sarah wanted to know.

"Probably eating for comfort," Tom suggested.

Dani put up the fifth grade photo.

"Oh my Lord," Sarah exclaimed. "Look at her eyes!"

Chelsie's eyes now had the vacant look. Her weight was worse. She was not the girl they knew.

"I want you to two to dig into the family," Sarah said to Macy and Tom. "I need to know what was going on and who was in this child's life. Leave no stone unturned. Talk to elementary teachers. Talk to childhood friends if you have to. I want to know what happened to make her this way."

"Wait," Macy interrupted, "I think Dani has more."

Sarah turned to Dani. "I have put excerpts from her journal in the folder. I have not been able to determine if she continued keeping a journal after she left the hospital."

"Then I'll draft a search warrant for her bedroom," Sarah said. "When we get it I want a copy sent to Miss Montgomery. She has been very insightful so far."

"Is there a chance I could talk to Chelsie?" Dani asked.

"You would be the only person outside her family, doctors, and lawyers to do so."

"Who has the best rapport with the mother?" Dani asked.

Tom answered, "Probably, Macy."

Dani turned to Macy, "Can you get me in to see her next week?"

"I'll do my best."

"Does anyone have anything else?" Sarah asked.

"I'm good," Tom answered.

"Me, too," was Macy's response.

Dani shook her head negatively and started picking up the things she brought. She took each photo off the board and put them back in her file. Sarah left the room and Tom said, "I'll meet you in the office." Then he left.

"Thanks, Dani," Macy said. "You've unearthed something we totally overlooked."

"Not really," Dani replied closing her briefcase. "If you had studied her medical records you'd have found it eventually."

The two of them left the room and headed for the stairs. Outside the courthouse they paused. "I'm off to set my first abused woman on the road to freedom. Call me when we can see Mrs. Patton."

"We?" Macy asked.

"Yes, I don't want to see her alone. I want someone to take notes and ask questions I might forget."

"I'll call when it's set up."

They hugged and Dani watched Macy walk toward the police station. Then she made her way to her car. Tossed her briefcase on the seat and called Margo.

"HELLO."

"Margo, it's Dani are you ready?"

"As ready as I'll ever be, I'm almost to the crossroads."

Dani smiled, "I'll be there in about three minutes. Pull into what used to be the general store."

"Sure thing, see you soon."

They hung up each heading to the crossroads where Dani would turn Margo over to the next person on her road to domestic freedom. This was a score for Michelle. *When Misty was passed on later tonight, it would be a second score.* Dani hoped Michelle was smiling in Heaven as she saw her friends working to prevent what happened to her from happening to anyone else. Moments later she spotted Margo's car in front of the old general store.

Getting out of her car, Dani approached Margo, who stepped out of her car. "You are going to leave the car, title and keys with me," Dani told her. "I'm going to sell it and the money will come to you or the people up the road will get you another car."

"I don't care what you do with it," Margo told her. "It was Evan's car. I only drove it with permission." She handed Dani the signed title, and keys, "I'd like to see the money go to Lizzy and her kids. They need it more than I do."

"As you wish. Do you want me to tell her?"

"Nope, just see they get whatever you can get for it."

Dani took the title and keys, "Consider it done."

"Thank you."

They watched as a van approached from the north. Dani could feel Margo's tension rise. She put a hand on her arm, "Get what you have in the car."

Margo leaned in and pulled out her purse and two medium sized suitcases. She also put on a backpack. By then the van had pulled in and stopped.

Dani approached the van, "Drop off to freedom?"

"Railroad ready to board," was the answer she got.

Margo hugged Dani while the driver stored her bags in the back. "Thank you again."

"You're welcome, I hope things turn out well for you."

Margo got into the van and the driver pulled out and headed north. Dani watched until they were out of sight. Then she locked Margo's car, made a call to Mason Towing, and waited for them to arrive. She directed them where to take it and headed for home.

On her way home Dani took a call. It was Macy. "Dani, we got the search warrant and found a box of journals."

"Whoa, I was just hoping she kept writing," Dani said. "Can you just have it messengered to me when you get it all copied?"

"I can do better," Macy sounded excited. "I got Sarah to put you on the payroll for this one and as long as you are willing to sign for it, I'll bring it within the hour."

"Great! I am about ten minutes from home, so I'll be waiting. Bring the appropriate paperwork."

"On my way."

Dani hung up she could hardly believe her luck. Temporary work with the Rivers County DA's office. A chance to help a victim of something and to help Macy. She pulled in at home, heard the laughter of Teddy and Amy floating on the air. She smiled, knowing once again, this was right and walked into her office.

"Miss Dani, how was your day?" Maureen asked smiling.

"It was interesting. Macy McVannel will be here shortly she's bringing me evidence from a case we're working on. Please send her right in."

"You are working with Rivers Edge Police?"

Dani stopped in her doorway, "I am on temporary assignment with the Rivers County DA's office. We are working on a case I've been read into."

"I understand, the one you got the medical records on."

"Yes," Dani confirmed. "We think the accused was a victim of something when she was young."

"Hopefully, you will be able to help them figure it out."

Nodding, Dani went into her office put the files from today's case in her out basket to be filed and took out the Chelsie Patton file. This was going to grow before she was done with it.

She heard a commotion in the outer office, Teddy and Amy arrived at her door. They were each carrying a tray. Amy's had cookies on it and Teddy was carefully balancing one with a mug and creamer on it. Dani took the one from Teddy.

"Thank you both for bringing me snacks," she told them as she turned to hug them both.

"We know you are going to Mr. Brad's for dinner tonight so we thought you might need something until then," Teddy told her.

"Are you okay with me going?"

"Mom told us it wasn't our business and if you and Mr. Brad were happy we should be happy for you," he answered. "Miss Dani, I do want you to be happy. I know Mom is."

"I'm glad, Teddy, because I want you, Amy, and your mom to be happy."

Teddy reached for Amy's hand, "C'mon, we need to let Miss Dani get her work done." They left hand-in-hand.

Dani put cream in her coffee and started water boiling so Macy could have tea when she arrived. Then she picked up a cookie, sat at her desk, and enjoyed a moment to herself.

The water was ready as Macy arrived. Dani was pouring her a cup of tea as she came in and sat down. Macy picked up a cookie as she waited for Dani to join her.

Dani handed her the cup of tea, closed the door, and sat at her desk. "Tell me how you convinced Sarah Stephens to put me on the payroll and make me part of this case."

Macy took a drink of tea to wash the cookie down then answered, "I pointed out the amount of time you'd put into the case already. As well as all the things you brought to the forefront. She agreed you had a stake in seeing it through to the end."

"Terrific! Do you have papers for me to sign?"

Macy dug into her bag to pull out papers for Dani to sign, they included a W-2 form, a confidentiality form, an agreement to work on behalf of the Rivers County DA's office, and a form for chain of custody. When Dani was done with the forms, Macy handed her the shield of the District Attorney's office and welcomed Dani to the team.

"I'm stunned," Dani told her. "Can we put off seeing Chelsie's mom until I've had a chance to read through the journals?"

"Call me when you're ready."

The two women enjoyed another cookie each and finished their drinks. Macy stood and so did Dani. The two friends hugged.

"I'll get back with you as soon as I can."

Macy nodded, "I know you will."

Dani walked Macy out, then went back to her office. "I'm done for the day Maureen. I have a couple other things to do before I go out to dinner."

"Is there anything you need me to do?"

"No, just have a great weekend."

"What about Margo Hunter's car?"

"I arranged to have it sold and they will messenger us a check." She lowered her voice, "Margo, wants the money to go to Lizzy and the kids. We'll just put it in an account and let it draw interest until it is time for them to leave. Oh, and I'm taking Lizzy on Monday to see about getting her into a walking cast and to see if we can get her scheduled for court."

"Sounds like a good plan. I'm off then. Have a nice weekend."

DANI CLOSED UP the office and went to see Ella. Ella had just finished making rolls to go with the crockpot dinner.

"Ella, did you have time to say good-bye to Misty?"

"Yes, child, I can't thank you enough for saving her."

"She won't be able to tell you where she is, but I have given her a way to get word to you."

Ella sniffed to keep tears from falling, "I hope she can find someone to love her and show her how wrong Rocky was."

"I think it will be a while before she becomes involved again," Dani assured her.

"It would be best if she waited," Ella agreed.

"Well, I need to change. Brad is coming up river for us." Dani gave Ella a hug then headed for her room. She changed into jeans, a t-shirt, sweater, and moccasins. Then slipped out of her room and into the linen closet and down the stairs toward where Misty waited.

She called out as she got closer, "I'm coming down."

"I'm here," Misty called back.

Dani found Misty sitting on the daybed reading. She chuckled, "Take the book with you."

Misty closed the book, "I was trying to get through it before I left. I made a challenge to myself to read as many as I could. I signed the back of each I read. This one is number five."

"Take it as a reminder of what you've been through and how you have a new start."

"I'd like to, is it time?"

Looking at her watch, Dani said, "We have about ten minutes. I don't want to leave before we absolutely have to."

"My stupid brother-in-laws?"

"No, I just don't want people finding the entrance."

"This will be hard for you as the years go on," Misty surmised. "I wonder how you will keep your own children from finding this place."

"Children?" Dani laughed. "I think I need to be married first."

"And I think it will happen sooner than you think."

"Time will tell." Dani checked her watch again. "Grab your stuff, we are on our way."

Misty picked up a bag Ella had given her and a small cooler. She also took the book Dani had offered.

As they made their way down the tunnel, Misty said, "I left you a list of the things I used."

"Thanks, I'll get them replaced." She unlocked the door and stepped out looking around. She heard Brad coming up river. "Go wait on the dock. I'll lock up here."

Misty quickly made her way to the dock trying to make herself as small as she could. Dusk was falling. Dani locked up and joined Misty on the dock. As Brad came into view Dani got ready to tie the boat off. She secured the boat and turned to Misty.

"It's time."

Misty came to stand beside her. Brad reached for her bag and cooler. After he stowed them away he helped Misty into the boat.

"I need you to move up front and hold onto the dock pole so I can help Dani into the boat."

Misty moved to the front and held onto the pole as if her life depended on it. Once Dani was in the boat, they sat beside each other. Sensing Misty's fear, Dani took her hand. Misty squeezed the hand in hers. She was worried her ex brothers-in-law would somehow find a way to stop her.

As they pulled into the marina, Misty tried to see if they were hiding somewhere but it was too dark to see much. Dani helped tie off the boat, then Brad helped her out. He handed her Misty's belongings and then lifted Misty out.

As Brad was climbing out, Dani led Misty to Brad's truck. Once in the back seat, Misty laid down.

"You can sit up," Dani told her. "It's no secret where we are going."

"I don't want to chance my brother-in-laws seeing me."

"Have it your way."

Brad climbed into the truck, looked quizzically at Dani who shrugged, started the engine, and set out on the short trip. It took them ten minutes to get to the truck stop off the expressway.

"Let's go get coffee," Brad said.

Misty sat up and they all went inside.

Brad found them a booth near the door and told the waitress to bring three coffees.

"How long do we have to wait?" Brad asked.

"I'm not sure," Dani answered. "It was about five minutes with Margo."

"Will it be the same person?"

"Again, I have no idea. They give me a coded sentence to listen for and one to repeat."

The waitress brought their coffees. They sipped while they waited. Misty seemed less anxious.

In less than five minutes, a woman approached them. She looked at Dani and asked, "Package for pick-up?"

"Cargo is ready," Dani replied.

"This way please," the woman said heading for the door. Dani and Margo followed. Brad threw some bills on the table and brought up the rear.

Outside the woman said, "Baggage."

"I'll get it," Brad volunteered. He went to his truck, grabbed the suitcase, backpack, and cooler.

They followed the woman to a semi. She helped Misty in the passenger seat, handed up her bags and said, "You can put them in the berth behind you."

Misty did as the woman went to the other side and climbed in. Brad and Dani stepped back so they rig could pull out. They watched until the rig turned south onto the expressway then walked to Brad's truck.

ON THE RIDE to Brad's he began with questions, "How did they know to approach you?"

"I told them there would be two women and a man. I also told them the blonde woman would be wearing a blue t-shirt with a navy sweater."

"Sneaky." Brad said but smiled at her. He put his arm around her. "I am amazed by you."

"You haven't heard the best part yet." She sat up straighter and told him about being a temporary employee of the Rivers County DA's office.

"Gee, am I going to ever get to spend time with you?"

She jabbed him in the ribs, "I still have my evenings free."

"Glad to know."

They drove on in silence as Dani snuggled in next to him. It was a feeling he loved.

They arrived and Brad poured Dani a glass of wine he had chilling. She took the glass.

"Go check out the stars from the deck," he suggested as he busied himself getting their dinner ready.

He had made meatballs and spaghetti sauce ahead of time. He just needed to boil the spaghetti and put the garlic bread in the oven. Then he joined Dani on the deck. He walked up behind her and slid his arms around her.

"This is beautiful."

"I'm glad you like it. Dinner will be ready in about eight minutes."

"What can I do to help?"

"Absolutely nothing. Dinner has been warming in the oven, it's now on the stove and the garlic bread is in. I set the table before I left."

She leaned into him, "I could get spoiled by this."

"What happened to the girl Ella was training?"

"She left when you were working in the chamber. Claimed she was not working in a haunted house."

Brad smiled above her head. His antics had worked. "I guess I haven't been too observant. I'm going to check the bread."

"I'll come with you."

Together they walked back inside the cabin. Brad served dinner and they cleaned up.

"I don't have anything exciting for dessert," Brad told her as they put the last dish away. "I do have something though."

Dani wrinkled her forehead as she looked at him.

"Will you go sit on the couch for a minute?"

"Sure, I guess." She made her way to the couch and sat. *What is he up to now?*

Brad came to her and handed her a bouquet of red roses. Dani took the roses putting them up to her nose to smell. It was then she noticed she was eye to eye with Brad.

"Dani Montgomery, I have loved you all my life. Would you do me the honor of becoming my wife?"

"Yes!"

He opened the ring case and slipped the diamond on her finger. "I asked Sam and Ella for their permission, since I couldn't ask your parents or grandparents."

"Oh, Brad." She set the flowers aside and threw herself into his arms.

ACKNOWLEDGMENTS

As always, my readers get my biggest thank you.
You continuing to ask for more, keeps me going.

My beta readers Donny Winter and Jen Evans helped me
polish up this one and make it a good read. Thank you both.

The superb staff at BHC Press have once again
made my work something to be proud of.

ABOUT THE AUTHOR

Retired teacher Rebecka Vigus spends her time writing, reading, crocheting, hiking, and swimming. She travels seeking the ideal place to call home. Ms. Vigus has been writing since she was in her pre-teens. Her first book was poetry, *Only a Start and Beyond*. Since then she has penned five, full-length novels, one book for children, several short stories, and even a self-help book for tweens and teens. Ms. Vigus has been listed as a Michigan Author and Illustrator at the State of Michigan website.